WINGS UPON THE NIGHT

By

JACK G. SALTER

To:

The mothers and fathers, wives and children and lady friends
of all those airmen who failed to return…

First published by the Author 2009
All rights reserved
ISBN 978-09555169-2-4
Printed and bound in the U.K. b y
Hobbs the Printers Ltd. Brunel Rd., Totton, Hants.

This book is sold subject to the condition that it
Shall not by way of trade or otherwise, be lent,
re-sold, hired out or otherwise circulated without
the publisher's prior consent in any form or binding
or cover other than in which it is published
and without a like condition including this condition
being imposed on the subsequent purchaser.

THE AUTHOR

Jack Salter was born and educated in Hampshire. On leaving school he trained as a aircraft engineer and also learnt to fly.

He has held several and various posts in industry and commerce over the years but flying, riding, writing and piano music have been the main focus of his attention throughout his life. And continues to this day.

He has two daughters and three grandsons and lives happily with his South African wife, Lincia, on the edge of the New Forest.

PROLOGUE

'Wings upon the Night' is a sequel to the author's 'War Pilot'.

The Second World War is in its third year and two of the Herby family have lost their lives to it.

Samantha, conceived by Samuel Herby and Claire Hadley, died from wounds received during a covert flying operation. And Paul, son of Timothy and Marie Herby, met his death when duelling, in an unarmed reconnaissance aircraft, with a Luftwaffe Messerschmitt in which the German officer also perished.

Samuel Herby, in Canada, received the news of Samantha's death from her mother, Lady Hadley, in a private and confidential letter sent to him at the flying school, to avoid offending his wife, Rebecca Herby.

He was still in the throes of grieving the loss of a daughter, he had never met, but with whom he had corresponded, when Timothy, his son, wrote with the devastating news of his grandson Paul's death on operations.

It was during the process of grieving for his daughter and grandson that Herby senior came face to face with the fact that the Herby name was in danger of fading out.

He wrote of his concerns to his son. But in all subsequent letters that Timothy wrote to him he refused to be drawn on the matter. Either he was embarrassed for whatever reasons, or, his son's responsibilities as a senior air force officer had the priority of his time over what was only an unimportant, sentimental family matter.

One

The small, overcrowded car threaded its way through the country lanes under a ragged moonlit sky, trailing a riot of song that almost drowned the sound of its labouring engine.

> 'Coming home on a wing and a prayer,
> For all of us boys we don't care,
> An engine 's shot away,
> We're just going to pray,
> We live to see another day.'

The voices roared again and again at the night air and hung on the moisture-swept breeze.

The singing stopped abruptly and sergeant Clarke shouted, "What are you doing down there Wally."

"Playing scrum half. What else do you expect boyo." the muffled Welsh accent came up from beneath his legs.

Sergeant Croker said: "Fart on him someone, and see how quick he gets out of the scrum."

Flying officer Fenton said, "Any more of that language and you can all walk home. What says you Bosey?

Flight sergeant Bosanquet, forced by the cramped conditions, sat hunched over the steering wheel, smiled in the darkness, "The lot of you might as well do that. I haven't a clue where we are."

"Leave it to Fenny," Clarke suggested. " He's the navigator in the crew."

Croker stumbled on a hiccup. "Fenny couldn't navigate a fart."

"I've helped bring you lot home from a raid often enough." Fenton said indignantly.

"You what!" Croker jibed. "From what Maurice tells us – you and the skipper hide under the chart table whilst the rest of us chase off the Jerry night fighters."

"Did somebody mention the skipper." the Welsh accent reached up again from the floor of the car. "Anyone for tennis?"

The comment immediately filled the car with a bout of unrestrained laughter.

"It's not the flak that worries me." Croker scorned. "It's his bloody night landings. When are you going to teach him to land the flaming thing, Bosey?"

Bosey nudged Fenton in the darkness, "The skipper has good reasons for doing those type of landings. Hasn't he Fenny? It's to shake off any loose shrapnel we may have picked up over the target."

"That's right."

"Anyone for tennis?" Croker mimicked the Welshman.

Another outburst of laughter filled the car.

The car paused at a junction, barely discernable by its shaded headlamps. And some delicate balancing of clutch and throttle were needed to get it under way again; it was grossly overloaded. But move it did and they crept along the road toward the aerodrome. During a brief silence from the seats behind him Bosey shouted, "Did you enjoy your birthday party, Davy?"

"Yes. Thanks a lot everybody! The best I've ever had."

Bosey said, "You may as well know the skipper chipped in with a fiver towards the food and drinks."

"Why did he leave the party early?" Clarke asked. "Does he find us coarse and rowdy at times?"

He didn't get an answer; Bosey was busy turning into the main gates of RAF Beeston and keeping the car going past the loitering service police. They dropped Fenny off at the officers' mess and continued to the sergeants' mess and parked in the shadows.

"Goodnight Bosey." Clarke yawned.

Wally swayed uneasily as he emerged from the car and attempted to straighten his crumpled uniform tunic and adjust his tie. The cold air heightened his intoxication. He leaned toward the pilot wagging a finger and in a slurred voice said, "Did anyone ever tell you, Bosey, that you fly a Halifax better than a Standard 8."

"Hey!" Croker shouted after Clarke. "Don't forget Eddy."

Edwards had drunk himself under the table long before the end of the party. They were forced to carry him to the car for the journey home. Now they had to drag him from the car and carry him upstairs to his bed: a journey that had all the makings of a good cabaret act.

Bosey lingered outside the mess after they had gone. He could feel a rising anger in the wind as it drove large fragments of cloud across the face of the moon. He debated on the chances of the weather improving for their next raid. For certain the skipper would not like to be attempting a landing on a night like this.

Flying Officer Hadley-Chase lay in the darkness of his room, hands behind his head, listening to the roller of the blackout blind chattering against the window frame. Details of the room repeatedly brightened and dimmed as the moon skimmed between the cloud breaks. He felt tense and harassed; his night landings were not improving. Throughout an entire operation his greatest anxiety was getting the Halifax back to earth in one piece, and without drawing the mirth and unwelcome comments from certain members of the crew. This weakness in his flying haunted him relentlessly.

He relived it again at this very moment: the flare path coming to view as he turned the Halifax onto the final approach. His body and thoughts recoiled like a spring. His hands and feet tensed on the controls. His fear was so acute he could barely hear the noise of the engines. The tapering runway lights drifted up in the confines of the windscreen, teasing him by drifting from side to side. He just could not get the nose to hold steady toward the lights. He called Bosey to put on a bit more flap. As the nose fell away he eased back a fraction on the control column and wound the trimmer wheel back a number of notches. In the last three hundred feet the lights seemed to race up at him.

"Anyone for tennis." the voice mocked him over the r/t.

He cringed. The first two lights swept by. He eased the control wheel back and slowly closed the throttles. The wheels never touch down when he expects them to. And just as he thinks they'll never touch ground the Halifax slammed into the concrete and rebounded like a scalded cat.

"One love!" that was Croker's voice.

The pilot pushed the control wheel forward. Should he open up and go round again? Did he have enough runway…the force of the impact squeezed him against the seat harness. He lost sight of the runway lights as the Halifax bounded into the air yet again.

"Two love!" Walters's Welsh accent sounded.

The pilot gripped the control wheel, stricken with fear, as the Halifax plunged.

"I've got her!" Bosey moved urgently beside him brushing his hands from the controls. The engines roared momentarily, Bosey pushed and snatched at the control wheel, three times in quick succession, and the heavy bomber checked itself and fell with unbelievable gentleness onto the runway.

"Game! Set and match!" Croker shouted jubilantly.

The scene faded and HC found himself gripping the sides of his bed. He moved to the window and stood smoking a cigarette with trembling fingers.

The problems with his night landings had followed him all the way through his flying training, starting with his second night solo in a Magister when he ran into a gooseneck flare and narrowly avoided setting the machine ablaze. His instructor passed it off as a training incident.

He fared little better when he moved on to flying the twin-engine Oxford. On his first night solo he ground looped on landing. Three flights later he hit the ground so hard he broke a radius rod on the undercarriage. It was ignored such were the desperate calls by operational squadrons for more pilots.

On being posted to an Operational Training Unit the size of the Halifax daunted him. And after a string of night landings, during which it was necessary for the instructor to intervene, he was taken aside and told, "If you think you can use your landings to work your ticket, you can think again!"

He later learnt that several aircrew on nearing the end of their operational training got cold feet when operational flying loomed. Evidently many faked up an excuse or developed undesirable traits in their flying in the hope they would be excluded from front-line operations.

For HC the veiled hint and suggestion he was a coward had an amusing irony about it. The instructors nagged and bullied him through the course.

His anxiety increased four-fold when he reported to his first operational squadron; he had no wish to kill his crew with a dodgy landing. It was rather odd how he ended up with a seasoned sergeant pilot as his second pilot when other crews only had a single pilot. But he was infinitely pleased and relieved that he had.

Their next raid, their thirteenth, was a couple of nights later. There were some misgivings about the weather forecast at the briefing. And when they drew near the runway for take-off Croker noticed large spots of rain falling on his rear turret. He grinned; with a bit of luck it would get worse and they'd get a recall signal. HC swung the Halifax onto the runway with rudder and a burst of engine, straightened it up and braked. "Captain to crew. Prepare to take-off."

Bosey tapped out their identification letters through the belly light. In response a steady green light glowed at them from the control van. HC pushed the throttles up the quadrant with his right hand whilst Bosey mounted guard with his left. A great crescendo of sound engulfed the entire machine – they began to move – each and every crew member tensed and trying to divert their thoughts from the hazards of the take-off with an aeroplane that was loaded to the maximum with bombs and fuel. A mistake by a pilot or a mechanical failure at the wrong moment and a violent death awaited them all.

The trundling Halifax got into her stride. The tail came up and she surged forward in the bellowing orchestra of her four growling Merlin engines.

"60 knots…70… 80..." Bosey called.

HC kept her down a bit longer; conforming to a tip from Bosey who claimed the extra speed made for more lift and better control if an engine failed during or just after take-off. He gave a steady heave on the control wheel – a pause – the rumbling wheels and the straining vibration stopped abruptly. He braked the wheels and Bosey selected undercarriage up. At a safe height he adjusted the boost and revs and the chaotic din of the engines fell to a more tolerable note. They banked eastwards to venture into the dark and dirty night. In the soft red glow of the instrument panel lights the rate of climb hovered around 600 feet per minute. The ball held steady in the turn and slip indicator, the figures on the directional gyro revolved slowly, and the image on the artificial horizon was slightly above the bar and tilted to the left.

Harvey Fenton came forward to check the course set on the compass after HC levelled the wings. And they sat growing cold in the laborious climb to 17,000 feet.

They had just crossed the coast when the wireless operator, Stan Sparks, received a transmission ordering the raid to be aborted and for all aircraft to return to base. He scribbled it on a message pad and went and handed it to the pilots.

HC peered through the windscreen at the dark and interminable night sky. He was in no doubt that they were flying into bad weather; for the last quarter hour the Halifax had rose and fell constantly and he had felt the jolts and tremors through the airframe from the turbulence.

He was also aware that they had been recalled four times in the last six weeks for the same reasons. Each cancellation meant another day added to their tour of operations and another day to debate on their chances of survival. It all added to the already frayed and tattered nerves.

He decided to press on and ignore the 'recall' signal. If he pulled it off it might earn him some respect from certain members of the crew and, in the process, reduce the scorn of his night landings. Bosey nodded in agreement when he suggested they press on and Harvey said it was worth a try. He did not ask the rest of the crew; he merely told them of the 'recall' signal and his intentions to carry on.

The pitching movements of the Halifax grew more pronounced the further they flew. Until they were lurching and stumbling through the stormy night, small and insignificant amongst the towering exploding cloud formations that lashed them with lightning, pounded them with hail stones and irritated them remorselessly with the crackle and hiss of the static electricity through the earphones of their leather helmets.

At times the broiling pressures and vortices of the storm sought to wrench them from the sky. Items of gear and equipment broke loose subjecting them to a perilous game of dodge and miss. It turned out to be a lot more ferocious than HC had bargained for. And if they didn't fly out of it soon he dreaded to think what might become of them all. It was as well that he had the loyal Bosey to fall back on. Sergeant Jaque Bosanquet who could be relied on to lend a hand in a crisis without the need of a compliment and who, with great discreetness, never let on to the rest of the crew. There he was, at this moment, reaching for the controls and the throttles to prevent the battered, nervous Halifax from succumbing to the elements.

Fenton had long stowed his maps, charts and plotting instruments. He was now debating whether his agreement to press on had been a wise one. But he reminded himself that he and the skipper were fellow officers and loyalty was of paramount importance in such situations. The Halifax was falling about all over the place, tossed like a cork on an ocean. He found himself bracing his legs and reaching out for support as the Halifax plunged and rose and banked and yawed. He'd never flown through anything like it before. And would never do so again if given the choice.

Walters sat in the nose, singing loudly into his muted r/t mask, pretending he wasn't afraid but wishing earnestly they'd fly out of it soon.

Corporal Clarke sat in the mid-upper turret hanging on to anything that gave him support. Young and enthusiastic he found it all rather amusing and exciting. He felt safe knowing Bosey was up front. For Bosey it was who had pulled them out of some narrow scrapes before. He thought Dave Croker and Wally Walters were quite hurtful in their snide remarks about the skipper. As far as Clarke was concerned the skipper treated him decently enough and, in recent weeks had recommended him for sergeant stripes.

That would be something to write home about. He laughed breathlessly as the Halifax dropped like a stone and the lap strap bit into his thighs. As suddenly a heavy unseen hand pressed him hard into the seat when the Halifax zoomed upwards. He wondered what Croker would be making of the present fiasco in the loneliness of the rear turret.

Perched in his rear turret on the end of the fuselage Croker was not amused. In fact if it went on much longer he'd be sick or dirty his underpants. Each movement of the Halifax greatly exaggerated his dipping and diving and his rolling and swaying such was the extremity of his position from the centre of gravity. He swung involuntarily through great arcs of movement, which seemed so severe to him he felt it would wrench the Halifax tail off and send him in a metal coffin to his grave.

It was one thing to stick your neck out against the flak and Jerry night fighters: the hazards of their occupation. But to die at the hands of bad weather or what he considered a useless pilot was not only unacceptable to him but he regarded it as a disgraceful way to die.

The young air gunner hailed from a deprived area of Liverpool and had a dreadful inferiority complex. The air force had brought him into contact, for the first time in his life, with the middle and upper classes. They spoke in a way he could not quite understand. Most of them sounded as if they had a plum stuck in their mouth or had their tongue wrapped around a glass marble. He got the impression they felt they were superior and when they spoke to you they looked down their noses and accepted you grudgingly. He regarded people like HC as snobs.

He did however like Bosey. He was a southerner but he had a different way about him. He talked in clear tones and to the point, and carried no airs and graces. If he disapproved of something he let you know in no uncertain terms as Croker had discovered when he arrived late for a briefing or left toffee wrappers strewn around his turret. Bosey was a great pilot and liked an orderly crew and aeroplane. What was more he always shook hands after delivering a reprimand to show there were no hard feelings?

At first the gunner thought it was his imagination. Then through the blindness of his fear he noticed the Halifax was flying in clear air. The rain and cloud had gone and up there before him stars twinkled on black velvet.

"Is everything all right back there, Davey?" Bosey's reassuring voice came over the r/t.

The gunner feinted a cheerful acknowledgement, took a toffee from a pocket, slipped it into his mouth behind his oxygen mask, and carefully disposed of the wrapper by wedging it in the top of a flying boot.

The pilots and navigator spent a number of minutes taking stock of the situation. Had the storm carried them far off course? Had the machine been damaged? All the gyro instruments had toppled and were slowly re-aligning.

"Searchlights!" Clarke called. "30 degrees to starboard."

"Just as well you eat your carrots each day, young Maurice." Bosey remarked, to be followed by a tumble of laughter over the r/t.

A distant rumble of thunder accompanied by a bright flash struck the air some miles ahead.

Walters said, "Old Fritz has got our height to a tee, Bosey. Keep an eye on him."

"Should we use the shell bursts as a target marker." HC said.

"As we don't know our exact position I don't think we got much choice. Did you hear that Wally?"

"I got you Bosey. But can I suggest we go in under the shell bursts. Make the run in at under 17,000 feet."

Another flash and explosion, much closer this time, ripped the black sky apart followed by a flurry of shell bursts.

"Action stations everyone." HC warned. "I'm starting the run-in now and descending to 15,000 feet."

Croker made certain his microphone was switched off and blew a raspberry into his mask in protest at HC's plum-cheek tone.

"Bomb doors open!"

A shell on either side of the nose cracked the air with menace. A marauding searchlight wavered before them, questing, taunting. Bosey pulled down his tinted goggles, a precaution he had learnt from experience during his first tour of operations.

Walters came on stage. "Right a bit…steady…steadeee…good. Left a shade…hold it…whoops! Right again…a bit more. Steady…steadeee…coming up to it now. Steady…steadeee…bombs gone!"

Almost simultaneously a stunning flash and explosion just above the port wing sent the Halifax down to the left into the blinding glare of a searchlight. HC abandoned the controls to shield his eyes. Bosey reached for the controls and the throttles and shouted: "I got her!" He reduced power but kept the Halifax diving in the hope the searchlight would think the machine was in a death plunge and would eventually divert its attention elsewhere.

The sudden lunge of the Halifax sent Walters full tilt over the bombsight. He lay awkwardly with his face pressed against the Perspex nose cone, completely unable to help himself.

Fenton sat wedged against his chart table. He caught a brief glimpse of Bosey reaching for the controls before the searchlight totally flooded the cockpit and blinded him.

Clarke fought down a surge of panic. From his position in the mid-upper turret it looked as if they were diving vertically and going down fast – very fast. Flickering clusters of light on the ground were looming and flak was sprouting up at them and getting very close. God! When were they going to pull out of the dive? He felt certain he could feel the heat of the carnage on the ground reaching up for his turret.

Croker sat with his back to the approaching earth, his hands gripping the gun handles in terror. The tail whipped about in all directions and shook constantly to the buffeting air of the dive. If they got an order to bale out he wouldn't have a chance in hell; he was trapped in his seat by the force and steepness of the descent. "I don't want to die." he murmured. Then a bit louder," I don't want to die." And when this met with no response he screamed, "I don't want to die!"

"Are you still with us Davey?" Bosey called cheerfully. And it was not until that moment that the gunner realised the Halifax was back on an even keel and they were turning away from the target.

"Just about Bosey. Just about." he said humbly.

"Right then, gents, we are still in one piece and on the way home. Keep your eyes peeled for night fighters."

They made the long weary flight back, unmolested, and dodged around the weather they had encountered on the outward trip by a combination of Bosey's piloting and Fenton's navigation skills. As they passed over the coast Bosey called the aerodrome to light the runway, and took the Halifax to ground.

Any crew knew that once a pilot turned the machine on to a dispersal pan the night's work was drawing to a close. Most important they were back in one piece and alive to tell the tale. In the rear turret Croker wiped the tears of relief from his eyes.

Two

When HC appeared before his senior officers the following day he knew his decision not to abort the raid would be high on the agenda. He had disobeyed the recall signal, he had put an expensive aeroplane at unnecessary risk and he had put the lives of his crew in jeopardy. He had also kept a lot of people up late to aid the landing of a solitary Halifax.

Harvey suggested he spin a yarn about the radio being duff. Bosey said it would save a lot of bother if he told the truth

"Morning Peter." Mellows his squadron commander greeted him cordially.

In complete contrast the group captain sitting next to him eyed him sternly. "Sit down." he said gruffly. "I think you should know that your flight and squadron commanders have, after a struggle, mark you, persuaded me to turn a blind eye to what happened last night. But I can tell you this – you won't get a medal for it."

The pilot discreetly nodded his thanks to Mellows who acknowledged it with a sly wink.

The group captain said, " I am, however, interested to know something about your crew. How would you rate them?"

"The fact we have completed thirteen operations must speak something of their calibre, sir."

"And how are your night landings coming along?"

The nerve was raw enough without the senior officer rubbing salt into the wound. He went on to the offensive. "As bad as they'll ever be. Nobody is perfect as you know full well, sir."

"I hear your night landings are a constant source of amusement amongst certain members of your crew."

The pilot deeply resented the second reference to his landings. "With respect, sir, that is a matter entirely between me and the crew."

After a pause the group captain said, "You have a gunner in your crew by the name of Croker. What's he like?"

"All right."

"Has he ever caused you any problems?"

"Not to speak of."

The senior officer leaned back in his chair gripping a pencil with two hands. "According to the Queen Bee, Croker is making an absolute pest of himself with the WAAFs on this station. She claims he has made seven of them pregnant and she reckons the air force is losing more back to civilian life than it can recruit. As his captain I think you should put him in his place."

HC said: "You must appreciate the private lives of my crew are no concern of mine unless, of course, it interferes with their work on operations."

"I might remind you, young man, that you have a duty to discipline any of the men under your command. You behave at times like a sergeant pilot."

"And I might remind you, sir! That pilots like flight sergeant Bosanquet, in my crew, are worth their weight in gold."

The group captain recoiled from the verbal slap in the face and said, "Very well. You've made your point. You may go."

In the pilot's absence he grinned. "He can't land an aeroplane at night. His crew is ribbing him something awful. And he won't have a word said against any of them. What a strange fellow?"

Mellows said: "I thought your references to his landings rather unfair."

"Really. I thought he handled it quite well. Nevertheless that is all beside the point. What are we going to do with this fellow Croker? Not a day passes without the Queen Bee comes to my office and bends my ear about this randy gunner."

Mellows smiled: "It doesn't help your case very much but I am of the opinion that the Queen Bee is getting too little of what Croker is getting to excess."

The group captain pushed a pile of papers into a brief case. "I'm obviously not going to get any sympathy here. So you can take me to the mess to get a double G and T and help me drown my sorrows."

Mellows winked at Forbes, "The most sensible thing I've heard today."

HC had something of a shock when he saw the Halifax in the light of day. The flight through the storm had blasted large areas of paint from the wings and fuselage leaving raw bare metal and rows of shiny rivet heads. The engines were running and Bosey was in the cockpit with an engine fitter, so said Harvey. HC led him away a short distance from the noise of the engines. "I know it wasn't popular amongst the crew, but thank you for backing up my decision to press on last night, Harvey. I'm most grateful to you." The navigator grinned at him. "Don't mention it, Peter. But between you and me I wouldn't rush to fly through anything like it again."

"Have you heard what the others thought of it?"

"Evidently Croker dirtied his underpants. And Walters had a go at Bosey, about it. In reply Bosey said it was only a mild storm; the wings and tail didn't drop off and the engines kept going; in other words you had done a grand job."

"The truth is Harvey it was Bosey who got us through last night. I totally lost it when that searchlight got us. In all honesty I think it's time I admitted I am not up to it as the rest of the crew know full well."

"Know what?"

"Come-come Harvey the crew know that I am carried by you and Bosey."

The navigator faced him squarely and compassionately. "Some captains lead by example, Peter. Others delegate responsibility. One might say you come within the latter category."

HC said: "Is that what some refer to as blind allegiance?"

"Possibly. Though I also think there are some who refer to it as the officer brotherhood."

Two nights later they were detailed for a raid on Hamburg, an unpopular target because it was heavily defended. Harvey Fenton, like most navigators, was methodical and followed a regular routine from the moment he attended the preliminary briefing for an air operation. He lay off tracks and measured distances and studied target photographs. Then after a brief chat with HC and Bosey he went up to his quarters after lunch and stretched out on his bed; the final briefing would be in about five hours.

He lay in the quiet privacy of the room visualising the legs out and back from the target and mulling over what could go wrong with the navigation and how he might best deal with it. From previous visits to Hamburg he recalled a number of good landmarks to aid the accuracy of his plotting. He also remembered a couple of spots along the route where the German night fighters had made a nuisance of themselves.

He suspected the winds given to them at briefing would be wildly different in reality. He couldn't recall when the met officer had last been correct. Would there be enough cloud to hide them from the night fighters? But not too much to prevent him using the sextant or the flame floats.

He closed his eyes and sighed. The challenges in his work were endless but not insurmountable. And he had his parents to thank for that. His father worked as a Stress Engineer at Vickers. His mother taught languages at the local grammar school. They owned a modest detached house in Kingston. A house that Harvey associated with peace and harmony and great chunks of learning, as one would expect from intellectual parents.

Harvey joined his father at Vickers when he left school and through showing a flair for technical drawing, and his father pulling a few strings, he got into the drawing office as a trainee draughtsman. To consolidate his enthusiasm he enrolled for evening classes at the local technical college.

He drew immense satisfaction from an idea originating in his head, then sketching it and finally producing a detailed drawing from which the engineers could manufacture the end product.

In his early days at Vickers such opportunities were rare however; he spent much of his time up dating or modifying old drawings.

He had finished his training and was waiting for his examination results to confirm he was qualified to receive the appropriate rate of pay when he got his calling-up papers.

His mother let him go begrudgingly. She and his father had spent a lot of money on his education and sustaining him on the meagre pay of a trainee draughtsman. And just as he was on the verge of qualifying and earning a decent salary the nation thrust him into a uniform and promises him an uncertain future. At least that was the way she saw it.

On the day he left home it was the first time Harvey had seen her moved to tears. Even at the very last moment she hung on to him straightening his tie, patting his hair into place and telling him not to forget to write.

The adjustment to life in the air force did not cause him any real problems. His background and education gave him direct entry as a commissioned officer. His training at the drawing board had prepared him well for the training as an air navigator. The plotting and the need for mental alacrity came readily to hand and so impressed were his instructors they suggested he should become an instructor at the end of his training.

He declined; the prospect of ending up in a classroom for the duration was not his way of fighting the war. He was young and wanted to be where the real action was.

It came soon enough when he was posted to an operational training unit and really got a taste of working in a confined space, in the chaotic din of four engines. Fighting off a cold that numbed his fingers slowed down his thought process and without fail chilled his hindquarters. He also got to know something about the distraction, tension and excitement of flying through the lethal flaming debris thrown up by the frantic defences of a target. The nervous anticipation of lurking night fighters. The ordeal of negotiating bad weather. And navigating an aeroplane back to its original point of departure.

Disaster struck on his final flight at the O.T.U. They were settling on the runway following a raid on Brest when the Stirling suddenly slipped and lurched to the left followed rapidly by a tooth-grinding crunch and harsh scraping of metal on concrete the victims being the port wing tip and outer engine propeller. Worse was to follow. The Stirling dug its nose in and flipped over onto its back and boomed and thundered in protest until it ground to a halt, inverted. Total confusion! Harvey fell in a crumpled heap against the roof of the Stirling. Next he was plunged into darkness. He had his first taste of panic; if a fire started he would burn to a frazzle. In no way could he get out!

A torch came on not far from him. He got himself standing with his feet on the inverted roof and noticed it was Stan Seaward, their wireless operator, trying to open an escape hatch in the side of the fuselage. It stubbornly refused to budge. Charlie Andrews, flight engineer, arrived on the scene, on his hands and knees, and with the aid of a crash axe they hacked their way out of the Stirling.

They stood at a distance from the wreckage not quite knowing what to do, dazed and rather shaken. They thought they saw ground personnel and vehicles arrive but when they called out nobody answered. Harvey lighted his pipe and handed the flickering match to Stan to light a cigarette.

"If you want to smoke, clear off!" a voice bawled at them in the darkness. "There could be fuel from a ruptured tank sluicing about your feet."

They retreated without any real sense of direction. Eventually a truck rounded them up and took them to debriefing.

They lost two of the crew that night. Tommy Gunther, tail gunner, broke his neck when the Stirling flipped onto its back and Harry Bradshaw, the skipper, perished with no apparent injuries. Looked as if he'd just fallen asleep, one of the medics said.

It was later suggested Harry had died from a heart attack caused by the shock of the catastrophic landing.

Within days Harvey received orders to proceed to his first operational squadron at Beeston 50 miles down the road. The decision to dispatch him evidently came at short notice; nobody at Beeston knew anything about him. The adjutant studied his identity card for a time then directed him to temporary accommodation in a transit block, and told him to report to the gymnasium in the morning.

The gymnasium echoed to a rowdy, disorderly mass of officers and NCOs who were attempting to follow instructions written on a large blackboard that said they were to form crews.

Harvey had barely arrived when, "What-ho there nav." He turned to find a sergeant pilot at his elbow. "Found your way into a crew yet?"

Harvey said: "I've just arrived."

"Good. Let's get cracking." the sergeant spear-headed a way through the mass of uniforms, and they came out on the fringes to find a young, awkward-looking officer, sporting a pilot's brevet, and looking completely overwhelmed with the situation.

The sergeant turned to Harvey. "The poor lad looks absolutely lost. Let's go and make his day."

They drew up before the unsuspecting officer. "How's your luck sir?" the sergeant said.

"Not very good as yet."

"Don't despair. I've brought you some. The navigator and I have nominated you as the captain of our crew."

After a round of introductions the sergeant led them back into the fray. They came upon a sergeant and corporal in deep conversation. Sergeant Bosanquet, noted the brevets on their tunics before he interrupted. "Are either of you in a crew yet? They shook their heads and he said, "You are now! Come and meet the skipper."

Another figure, wearing a gunner's brevet, tried to force his way past them. Sergeant Bosanquet grabbed his arm. "And where might you be going, young man?"

"I'm looking for pilot officer Cope."

"What for?"

"I hear he wants a tail gunner."

"So do we. You're in."

"Am I?" the bewildered youth frowned.

"You are. And what is more there is a chance you'll live longer. Just look at this fine bunch of men you'll be flying with."

Sergeant Croker was introduced to the others and thus completed the assembling of the crew.

Harvey was quietly amused by the way Bosey had rounded them up and by his cheerful driving force had moulded them into something of a team. It was rather odd why their crew had two pilots when others only had one. But it was fortunate for them all that they did; any of HC's night landings might easily have killed them all by now.

HC's predicament was somewhat sad. Peter was a genuine sort of bloke whose quality of speech suggested he came from a good background and had had a decent education despite the fact he very occasionally dropped his H's and exaggerated his A's. Probably came from mixed parentage. What was more he displayed all the masculine traits of a man but portrayed the slim anatomy of a woman inherited, no doubt, from his mother? And to crown it all, apart from his night landings, he was a good steady pilot. He had something to learn about leadership. But then he wasn't alone in this respect.

As another part in the routine leading up to a raid Harvey drew the curtains, set the alarm clock and slept for an hour. After which he took a bath to relax. Then down the mess for tea. And later up to the locker room to dress for flight and on to the final briefing.

Come on Fenny." Croker nudged him as they came out of the briefing room. "We can't leave you behind."

"Don't worry about Fenny." Walters shouted from behind. "I've sent our Maurice to the control van with a piece of string in case we get lost."

"Cigarette ends glowed as they helped each other into the waiting trucks which ferried them out to the aircraft. Later someone cracked a joke about the WAAF driver who had trouble finding the gears and they fell forward as a mass to the front of the truck – and back again – several times. They came to an abrupt halt at the aircraft, ending up in a heap at the front of the truck. And whilst they cursed and moaned and disentangled themselves the driver smiled revenge at Croker in the crew. She had told him she was expecting his baby and he point blank refused to accept he was the father, claiming she had slept with other men.

Fenny was the last to climb through the hatch into the Halifax and as he did so a girlish voice shouted from the truck. "I hope a German shoots your balls off, Croker!"

"Charming!" Fenton said as he closed the hatch and made his way to his office.

He spent time arranging his maps and tying his plotting instruments to the chart table. He used a handkerchief to polish the glasses on his small instrument panel. The four engines came to life in turn cocooning him in a constant train of vibration and the pounding beat of the engines that was magnified by the hollowness of the fuselage. Peter called them in turn to check the radio. Then they were trundling in the stream of aircraft to the runway.

The pilots did the take-off checks. Peter warned them to prepare for take-off and, after getting a green from the control van, they swung onto the runway. Presently the pilots unleashed the power of the engines. To the navigator it was both exhilarating and dangerous the more they accelerated. He had every confidence in Bosey's and Peter's handling of the Halifax but the majority of accidents happened during take-off. A lot of good pilots perished this way. He looked up front to see Peter holding the control wheel with both hands whilst Bosey held the throttles wide open and called out their increasing speed. The noise of the engines was almost hysterical; if an engine failed at this moment they would be in deep trouble.

Suddenly, lift came to the wings and hoisted them into the air. The end of the runway lights disappeared beneath the nose. On cue Bosey got the wheels up. Shortly after, the berserk, racing engines fell to a more gentle tone and beat as the boost and revs were adjusted for the climb. They turned on course and Harvey moved forward to check the course set on the compass by the pilots.

Half an hour later Walters, sitting in the nose, announced they were crossing the coast. Harvey uncorked his dividers and calculated their ground speed both mentally and with his Dalton. He always double-checked his calculations; it had formed part of his navigator training. Although in fact it had been ingrained in him from the start of his days in the drawing office.

The new information enabled him to work out a new ETA for the Dutch coast which he passed on to the pilots. In the light of a small porpoise lamp he looked down with satisfaction at the neat lines and symbols he had drawn on his Mercators chart. Pencil lines with arrowheads depicted the aircraft's track and true course and the symbols marked its air and ground position. A line marked with three arrowheads showed the wind vector.

Since there was little else to do at this stage he went and stood behind the two pilots. It helped to restore the circulation in his hindquarters; they suffered miserably from the chilled temperatures of the lofty altitude at which they flew. Way beneath them the North Sea heaved and swelled unseen. Occasionally the windscreen filled with a gathering of stars. At times they flew above a vast pale plain of cloud. At one stage they smashed soundlessly through the fringes of a heaped cumulus. From time to time Bosey spoke briefly to the gunners in the remote mid upper and tail turret.

"Coast line ahead skipper." Walters called from the nose. "The Hook is coming up on the port side. We're about 3 miles off track, Fenny."

Harvey moved back to his chart table and fixed their new position on the Mercator chart. His subsequent plots indicated the wind had backed and picked up a bit of speed. Nothing too dramatic but if left unchallenged could result in a substantial error over the distance they were travelling. He gave the pilots a new ETA for the target.

When they reached the target area Walters said: "That's bloody funny. We're about 8 miles off track."

Ahead of them lay a small cluster of lights. Over to their left fires raged upon the ground in the manner of a target that had already received a delivery of bombs. The other Halifax aircraft around them began to bank towards the scourge of fires. HC started to follow.

"Hold your horses!" Bosey shouted. "Keep to the original course." he reached across and swung the control wheel over, keeping a good lookout to ensure they did not collide with other aircraft changing course around them.

"I don't understand." HC stammered. "What's going on?"

Bosey ordered Walters to get to the bombsight and bomb on the small cluster of lights dead ahead.

"Those fires to port are a decoy." he explained to HC. "And are intended to lure us away from the main target. Do you see – there's not a burst of flak or a searchlight in sight in that area."

HC seemed a bit slow to catch on. Walters got him busy flying up to the target. Over to the left the fires were growing in intensity as the others rained down their bombs. And still no signs of a bursting shell or searchlight.

"Bombs gone!" Walters shouted.

"Close bomb doors." HC called.

Bosey closed the bomb doors and said: "Open up the taps, put her in a shallow dive, pull her around to the right and wait for it." The others thought they heard him chuckle. And before they had a chance to ask, 'wait for what' a great salvo of shells and searchlight beams sprang up around them.

"Bloody hell! Where'd that lot come from." Walters shouted.

"It could be a lot worst." Bosey pointed out. "And we might have collided with the main force if we had pulled round to the left."

The city of Hamburg suffered negligible damage that night and but for Bosey's quick thinking might have escaped totally unscathed. The decoy fires did considerable damage to the surrounding countryside without loss of human life. Though it was some time before Bomber Command got to know about it.

Before long the Halifax, remote from the main force, was on its way home. Harvey got the pilots to get above cloud and busied himself with a sextant. He had timed the shots of Polaris and Arcturus and was in the process of making his calculations when Walters announced he had got a visual fix on the Ems canal. Harvey plotted the astro position lines and was pleased to see they coincided with Walters's visual fix. It proved he could still use a sextant and the fix also proved the wind had not changed.

He got up to relieve his numbing posterior by rubbing it for a spell. The pilots told him when they passed over Den Helder and the West Frisian Islands. From hereon it would be a long haul across the North Sea. He checked all the information on his plot, filled in the navigation log and told the pilots he was putting his feet up and intended to have a swig of tea from his thermos.

After a very long r/t silence Walters shouted: "What was that?"

"What was what?" Clark the mid-upper gunner said nervously.

"I thought I saw something flash by under the nose."

"What was it like?"

There was a long pause before Walters cried out: " Long and fat like Croker's plonker."

"Don't be vulgar." Croker joined in. "Start rolling the string out Maurice. I think we're lost,"

Bosey ever wary of colliding with another aircraft or being pounced on by a lurking German night fighter said: "Right! Settle down and keep your eyes peeled. I'll string all of you up if a Jerry fighter takes a swipe at us, or, we collide with one of our own aircraft."

An hour later they crossed the coast. The pilots changed seats for the landing.

"Anyone for tennis" Walters called as the nose swung around to line up with the runway lights. Harvey smiled; Walters and Croker were in for a surprise, unaware that Bosey was at the controls. The Halifax drifted down the approach with full flap, engines pounding leisurely. They passed over the boundary and they all felt the Halifax check itself. Walters in the nose and Croker in the tail waited expectantly for the first jolt with the runway to send them back into the air. Instead they barely heard the squeal of the tyres when Bosey settled the heavy bomber between the lights in a classical three-point landing. Harvey deeply admired him not only for his skillful landing but for also sparing Peter from the scorn of Walters and Croker.

Of the many pleasures he enjoyed, following the completion of a raid, it was climbing down the hatch ladder and feeling solid ground beneath the soles of his flying boots. It came as a guarantee that they were home safe and sound and he could relax from his responsibilities.

There was quite a discussion at the debriefing concerning the decoy target. The intelligence boys didn't want to accept Bosey's idea that there was such a thing and his claim that his proof was based on the total lack of ground defences and searchlights in the area of the decoy target which soon disclosed themselves when he bombed the correct target. Harvey suspected the intelligence officers were too embarrassed to report to group that only one solitary Halifax bombed Hamburg and the rest of the force pounded half a dozen fields some 10 miles on the outskirts of the city. He backed up Bosey by saying the accuracy of the navigation both to Germany and back home proved, in his opinion, they had selected the correct target. And he had every confidence that if aerial photographs, taken in daylight, were made available it would prove Bosey's claim without an element of doubt.

The debriefing officer ignored it and said they were free to go. Harvey made his way furtively to a corner of the room where a certain WAAF stood by a metal tea urn. He gave her a sly wink and she secretly took his thermos, rinsed it out and filled it with fresh tea. She also slipped him a paper bag containing a couple of currant buns, which he slid beneath his flying jacket.

In his quarters he was able to shut himself off from the world. It had been a good night's work and he was satisfied with the part he had played in contributing to its success. He removed his flying jacket and hung it on a hanger on the door of a small wardrobe, pulled off a white roll neck sweater, and rinsed his face and hands. Of course there was a certain amount of luck in any of the bombing operations; he was well aware of that. They had got back safely. By morning he would hear of aircraft and crews who had not been so lucky.

Tired as he was after getting back from a raid he always found it difficult to fall asleep; his brain seemed to free-wheel and he needed to wind down slowly. He revelled in the simple pleasure of nibbling at the buns that he dunked in the tea. He followed this by lighting his pipe and sitting back and enjoying the uninterrupted tranquility of the night. Then from a drawer of a bedside locker he took a writing pad and pen and wrote to his parents. And to Kate who lived next door.

Three

Bosey cycled leisurely along the perimeter track of the aerodrome, heading for D-Dog. It was approaching midday. The air smelt fresh and the overhead sun brought a welcome warmth and brightness to the world. The previous night's operation had been a little dicey and they narrowly avoided a disaster. Occasionally a car drew level with him, containing another pilot making his way to a dispersal point and who offered him a tow. Today – he declined; he was in no hurry and he needed the exercise. He waved the cars on with his thanks.

Another car approached from the rear, sounded its horn, and swept past missing him by inches. "Move over sergeant! You're taking up all the road." Bosey recognised the big green Bentley as belonging to Flight Lieutenant Hawker, a flight commander. A regular air force officer with the push and initiative of Cranwell behind him. He was terribly plum-cheek and all that, with a good bit of the rebel in him. He allowed his hair to grow long and curl over his shirt and jacket collars. But he was a great character and competent pilot, idolised by his crew, and, in return, they could do no wrong in his eyes.

Bosey cycled past a forlorn looking Halifax, sagging on its undercarriage and minus its port outer engine, which had fallen out on a raid three nights ago. There was talk that the pilot and engineer of T-Tommy were to get a gong.

He came upon the battle-beaten shape of S-Sugar and thought of Tony Hooper its skipper who was always bleating about the Halifax's lack of power. Which was a trait of all Mk. 1 versions of the Halifax and of which most captains were aware.

The real problem arose from the fact that more and more equipment had been added to the Halifax since it became operational and yet nobody had thought to increase the power of the engines to cope with the additional weight. There was talk of getting rid of the mid-upper turret and other bits of equipment to reduce its weight in a bid to increase its operational ceiling. A rumour, also going around, said the black paint used on the aircraft was so rough it created a lot of unwanted drag. There was also the mumbling and grumbling about a large number of unexplained crashes. From what Bosey could gather from visiting Handley Page engineers the big heavy bombers were spinning in, inadvertently.

The engineers were of the opinion that the twin rudders were locking over and denying the pilot any chance of affecting a recovery.

But in spite of all this Tony's grand lady of the night was well into her second tour of operations, as the rows of bombs painted beneath the Perspex windows of the cockpit proudly demonstrated.

Bosey thought of D-Dog, the Halifax he flew. They'd flown their seventeenth operation in her last night and it had been plagued with problems from start to finish. The port outer engine overheated and they were forced to shut it down. And that was before they reached the target. On the homeward leg the starboard outer developed such severe vibration that too had to be shut down. "You'd better work out a new ETA for base, Harvey. And you, Eddy, have a look at our range and endurance."

"Watch out!" Croker's alarmed voice sounded. "There's another kite right up our rear end."

Bosey leant forward and switched the navigation lights on. He thought he heard the chatter of guns.

"Dive Bosey! The bastard 's firing at us."

HC hesitated. Bosey reached across, pushed the control column forward and drew the throttles back on the surviving engines. In a matter of seconds Walters bawled, "Ease off!" then much louder, "Ease off Bosey! There's another kite just below the nose."

Bosey tugged at HC's arm to get out of the seat and took his place. He applied power on the surviving engines. "How is it back there Davey?"

"I'm not sure. I think he climbed over the top of us. I'm pretty certain it was a Halibag."

"What's the score with you Wally?"

"He's a couple of hundred feet below and pulling ahead of us."

In the privacy of the darkness Bosey sighed. He often thought there were as many machines lost to collisions as there were to enemy action. The big wigs called for saturation bombing in tight formations but did not take into account that if one aircraft got a hit from a shell it could blow nearby aircraft to smithereens. What was more, inexperienced pilots could easily misjudge speeds and the separation from other aircraft demanded of them. And whoever took into account what would happen if a lame duck, such as themselves, interfered with the running of an operation in the poor visibility of a night sky.

Harvey came forward with a new ETA for Beeston. Eddy came on the r/t next and said they could increases their range by flying low and slow. HC argued they would be placed in a precarious situation if they flew too low and lost a third engine. They'd end up in the drink before they had a chance to organise the dinghy.

Bosey said, "If we potter around up here much longer we'll burn the fuel and be forced to ditch without a choice." He had delved quite a lot into the question of range and endurance when on his first tour of operations on Whitleys. A lot of pilots had run out of fuel by being sent to targets out of their range and capability by inexperienced operation planners. Or pilots were ignorant of the prudent use of the engine mixture controls.

After a brief exchange with Eddy regarding the fuel contents and tank selectors he took the Halifax down to a thousand feet and they began the long slow flight home. It seemed an age before they got across Holland. Then they left dry land and began to wing over the North Sea, all of them very conscious that if another engine gave up the ghost there would be precious time to get them out of the aeroplane into the dinghy. For a time the sky cleared and the stars were visible and in certain areas reflected their twinkling on the desolate expanse of sea.

At long last Walters shouted: "Coast ahead!"

"Thank God for that." Croker followed.

They'd soon be home. But as they flew further inland they came upon a blanket of fog that extended to the aerodrome and Beeston was diverting all aircraft some fifty miles down the coast.

"Beeston D-Dog from the east. Two engines feathered. Fuel critical. Request straight in."

"D-Dog this is Beeston. Negative. We have zero visibility in fog. Contact Nighthawk for diversion."

"Beeston I say again our fuel is critical."

There was a long pause before Beeston said: "Suggest you head out to sea and bale out."

"Negative!" Bosey hit back forcibly. " Request you give me the Queenie Fox Easy and the homer frequency."

Presently he was conversing with the homer operator, transmitting and receiving a succession of bearings, which he used to position the Halifax for the let down and approach to the aerodrome. He sank into the murk flying by instruments and continuing his transmitting to, and receiving bearings from, the homer.

Walters lay confronted by the opaque Perspex nose cone. It attacked him with waves of claustrophobia and reminded him of his training days on the ancient Overstrands when he was totally cut off from the rest of the crew and was always fearful of a machine smashing its nose in on landing. More recently there had been some nasty accidents when pilots tried to pit their skills against the clamping authority of fog – blind landings. If he had known HC was attempting this landing he would have baled out without telling anyone.

Fenton stood behind and between the two pilots hoping to assist in any way he could which wasn't much. He merely helped as another pair of eyes to prevent them banging into something. Bosey sat to the left of him looking intently at the instrument panel and occasionally making minor adjustments to the flying controls, the engine throttles and the trimmers. HC sat to the right, hunched, motionless, in the soft red glow of the instrument panel lights.

Clarke looked around at the uninterrupted gloom surrounding his mid upper turret. He felt confident Bosey had everything under control. There was just the worry another engine might pack up on them or they'd run out of juice. He didn't know why but he kept thinking about his mum and dad.

Croker compared his view from the rear turret to how it might look if he was sat in a bowl of dirty milk. In all the situations he could find himself he felt his chances of survival were better than the rest of the crew if they hit ground when they shouldn't. In a lot of prangs the rear fuselage broke off allowing the rear turret to escape the potential of a fire up front.

After another bearing from the homer Bosey swung the Halifax slowly onto the final approach. He called for another bearing to confirm he was heading directly toward the runway and punched the stop watch. The second hand began its jerky motion. He urged the bomber into a steady descent and adjusted the power and trim. Going in from a thousand feet, at 2 miles a minute, they should, given a helpful hand of luck, live to see another day. They had at least set the altimeter to the aerodrome pressure before they changed frequency to the homer, an oversight that had brought many a good crew to grief in the past.

Bosey called for a third flap. The airspeed fell away and he checked their descent by sliding on more power.

"Three hundred feet. Still blind." HC called.

Bosey nodded.

The big needle of the altimeter dropped below two hundred feet. "Still blind." HC called.

Bosey stirred. He slid on a bit more power, eased the nose up a fraction and wound the trimmer back a couple of notches.

The altimeter needle jerked below fifty feet; there was no guarantee of its accuracy from hereon. Five seconds to go on the stopwatch. "Standby everyone. And hold on to your seats," Bosey called. It was now or never. He drew the throttles back smoothly and eased the control column towards him. The airspeed fell to 90...80... the Halifax lurched onto the concrete, skipped feebly and settled. The fog was so dense he couldn't see the ground.

"Are we on the runway?"

"I think so," Walters replied. "I can see some watery lights going by on either side. Take it steady, Bosey, you're swinging to the right."

Bosey groped his way to the end of the runway turned onto the perimeter track, parked the Halifax and told control to send a truck to pick them up. The driver of the truck got lost in the fog; they got into the debriefing an hour after they had landed.

They were the only crew at the debriefing; 23 other aircraft from the station were diverted to other aerodromes unhindered by fog.

When they got to the sergeants mess, after the debriefing, they exchanged farewells as they made their way along the top landing to their bedrooms and Walters added, "By the way, Bosey. Thanks."

The pilot paused, turned and said, "Thanks? For what?"

Walters said: "For getting us down in one piece."

Croker said: "That goes for me as well, Bosey."

"And me!" Clarke and Edwards chorused.

Bosey grinned, "Don't thank me! Now get to your beds and don't forget to say your prayers."

He went to his room, smiling, switched the light on and plugged a kettle into a double socket he had unofficially rigged up with the ceiling light. He kicked off his boots and unwound his old, long woolen school scarf that he always wore on the raids, removed his battle dress top, hauled off a roll neck sweater, lighted a cigarette and, presently, sat enjoying a mug of tea.

Much as he enjoyed flying he was relieved that the night's work was over; he didn't want to make a habit of landing on two engines, in fog, and with only a couple of cupfuls of fuel sloshing around in the tanks. Some might regard his effort that night as a good bit of flying. Whereas he did not delude himself in thinking that it had been nothing less than dicey. Very dicey. They had been incredibly lucky.

It all combined to remind him of an incident that happened in February 1941 when he was flying Whitleys. They'd carried out a raid on Bremen and returned to England to find a whole host of aerodromes were 'Fogus Clampus'. There were no aids or procedures to bring an aircraft down in fog, in those days, and twenty-two crews were told to climb to a decent height, abandon their aircraft, and parachute to earth.

Bosey recalled that he had deserted his Whitley with regret. He still regretted it to this day. He grew attached to any aeroplane he flew. The rather slow and ponderous Whitley who the crew christened Gertrude, and who they referred to, affectionately, as Gertie, was somewhat eccentric in the way she flew. And yet night after night she flew against the stars and a variety of targets, collecting ice on her wings, and gasping and coughing when the ice formed on the engine air intakes. She dawdled up to a target hardly flinching at the German ground defences, perhaps bucking and shying now and then to confuse the guns and searchlights. On other occasions she kept her head down and flexed her wings like an actress spreading her arms and taking a bow at the theatre before a dramatic and spectacular firework display that was in reality the target

Not once did she fail to bring him and the crew back home, unharmed. And that's what caused the most grief and pain on the night they all abandoned her.

He learnt in subsequent days that she had returned to earth that night some sixteen miles away, landing on a country estate, on her belly, nose poised and did so, so decorously, that she incurred little damage. They gave her new propellers, replaced a few panels, beat out dents of others, treated a number of abrasions and scratches, gave her a fresh coat of paint and sent her off to an operational training unit.

As he cycled around the aerodrome the strong sunshine drew off the remaining lingering veils of mist and he discovered D-Dog that he had abandoned in the fog had been towed to the hangar and work had already started on the two duff engines.

"What's the score, chief?" he asked the sergeant heading the ground crew.

"Couldn't find anything with the overheating of the port outer you mentioned in the note left in the cockpit. I'm having the cylinder head temperature gauge replaced. How high did it go last night?"

"Nearly off the gauge. That's why I shut it down."

" Well I ran it this morning, and it ran quite sweetly. Have a go later."

"I will. What's the story on the starboard outer?"

"I had new plugs put in. And they are now changing the starboard magneto; it was showing a massive drop."

HC and Fenton arrived whilst they were chatting, followed presently by the rest of the crew. Edwards did not exactly agree with the sergeant, ground crew, regarding the port outer engine. From the running of the engine in flight he felt a big end had gone and that the filters should be dropped to check for metal droppings.

He was to be proved right, subsequently. The engine did not run well. The filters were dropped and bits from the journals of the big ends in the engine were found in the filters. The engine had to be changed. And Bosey went to Mellows, his squadron commander, and suggested the crew take a spot of leave whilst the job was completed. They were over half way through the tour and as yet had not had a break.

Four

The solitary figure of Hadley-Chase stepped from the train at Chad in the West Country a little after eight in the darkness of a winter evening. Old Topper the porter – cum- ticket collector grabbed the pilot's ticket in the shielded lighting of the ticket office but made no attempt to recognise him.

Outside the small halt the pilot rummaged in his great coat pockets for his pipe and matches. He got it alight, inhaled deeply and exhaled a long stream of smoke in celebration and relief at getting away from his air force responsibilities for a spell. He straightened up as if a heavy weight had been removed from his shoulders. Overhead an orderly display of stars stretched out across the sky and sparkled as a chain of diamond necklaces.

He pulled the large collar of his coat up around his ears to ward off the chilling night air, and set off down station hill past a gathering of cottages. He came upon the blacked-out windows of the Cock and Arrow. His mind went back to the pre-war days when Horace brought the farm hands and their wives for a generous supper, at his expense, to the public house to show his appreciation for them bringing the harvest safely in.

The hunched figure of constable Higgins crept past on his creaking bicycle and suddenly turned off and disappeared in the shadows at the rear of the pub to collect his customary tot of whisky from the landlord. It was to bribe him to turn a blind eye to the closing hours. Higgins always proceeded upon his habit quite certain it went unnoticed by the rest of the village. Whereas, in fact, the whole village knew about it, but didn't let on.

Some ten minutes later the pilot left the village and strolled along the dark, winding, unlit country lanes. He was speculating on how his mother would react to his unannounced home-coming when the drone of aircraft engines sounded behind and to the south of him. He paid them scant attention until air raid sirens began to wail their lament and out of the corner of an eye to the west he spotted pencil beams of light from searchlights swaying and rallying against the darkness of the night. He was in no doubt that Plymouth was the intended target of the German raiders.

Presently the horizon crashed and shook to the ferocious barking of the heavy guns and the torrent of falling, exploding bombs. Within minutes the devastation showed as a huge glowing pimple etched on the distant horizon and against the background of the night sky.

He walked on knowing he should be enraged by the dastardly deeds of the German bombers. But long after they had retreated, the guns silenced and the searchlights snuffed, he was only too conscious that he too went on bombing raids and he too killed women and children. He tried not to think about it too deeply. But he was not totally successful.

As he approached the gate of the farmhouse a slight drift of cow manure and hay greeted him. This was home and where he had spent much of his life – a happy and healthy life. God! It was great to be home. The dogs barked on sensing his presence and hearing him lift the gate latch. They came to him in the darkness wagging their tails and rubbing their cold velvety noses against his hand in greeting. A door opened sending a shaft of light along the cobbled yard

"It's all right. It's only me," he called.

"Goodness gracious! It's Peter. Come along in m' boy. Poor old Plymouth had another visit earlier."

The pilot squeezed through the doorframe, encumbered as he was with his kit bag, respirator and tin hat.

"Peter!" his mother rushed to greet him in the hall. "You might have told us you were coming." she hugged him excitedly.

"Mother! Was it not you who told me that all ladies thrive on surprises?"

"Yes," she laughed and fussed about him taking his topcoat and gear and hanging it in the hall.

She turned and checked him. "I'd better warn you before we go through that we have a guest. She's a girl from the land army and has been sent to help out on the farm. She's quite sweet isn't she Horace?"

Out of the corner of his mouth Horace said: "Pretty, but as dim as the rest of them. She can't tell an ear of wheat from a duck's rear end."

They moved into the sitting room greeted by the homely smells of smoked ham, baked bread, honey and a slight trace of wood smoke from the log fire in the large hearth. A young woman, sitting on a settee, rose to meet them as they entered and was introduced to him by his mother as Jenny. He was drawn immediately to her short fair hair, her distinctive green eyes and her delightful girlish smile. They had no sooner shook hands when his mother whisked her away to the kitchen to prepare him a snack.

In their absence he kicked off his shoes and stood with his back to the heat of the hearth. He told Horace what a comfort it was to feel the heat eating into his legs and posterior. His hindquarters and limbs always felt the cold during the bombing raids on Germany. And rarely thawed out before they set out on the next operation. He knew Harvey Fenton suffered the same privations. He considered what he was enjoying at this moment in time as a pure luxury.

"You must try a pair of long-johns." Horace suggested.

"I think you might be right, Horace." His feet got so numb at times on the raids he had a job to feel the rudder pedals.

The women returned, each carrying a laden tray, one of which was exclusively for him bearing a bowl of ham and lentil soup, a pile of ham sandwiches and a mug of Ovaltine.

Not having had leave since he started on operations at Beeston his mother was keen to know how he had fared. Gratefully she did not refer to his night landings, which he had told her about during his time in training. He spent a few minutes telling them about his splendid crew. The cheerful, dependable Bosey who displayed all the traits of an Englishman but whose real name was Jaque Bosanquet. Then there was his navigator and fellow officer Harvey Fenton who took them with great accuracy to a target and navigated them safely home, all under the cover of darkness. He had a young man from Doncaster, Maurice Clarke, who manned the mid upper turret. His bombaimer was a quick-thinking Welshman, and his rear gunner, from Liverpool, spoke with such a strange dialect it was very difficult to understand him at times.

The conversation changed to the raids on Plymouth, and then how the farm was progressing under the constant demands of the Ministry of Agriculture.

Like all farming families they retired early on account of having to start the day early. HC lay awake for a considerable time savouring the warmth and security of his bed, reassured that nobody could reach him here and drag him off in to the cold, dark night to drop the wretched bombs. Neither did he have to worry about the long haul home and face the nightmare of a landing in the dark.

It suddenly occurred to him that Jenny was in her bed on the other side of his bedroom wall. He drifted into sleep, imagining she was sharing his bed and he was holding her hand.

He awoke to the sight of his illuminated bedside lamp and Jenny standing there carrying a tray of breakfast. As she bent over to place the tray on his bedside table he caught sight of her plump young breast, revealed, as they were, when the collar of her dressing gown sagged.

Quite unable to resist the temptation he pulled her onto the bed, gripped her with his arms and attempted to kiss her. She squirmed, issued a muffled cry, and frantically pulled herself away from him. It was the fearful look in her eyes that persuaded him to release her. She hurried from the room in great haste. He fell back on the pillow smarting from the realisation of what he had done.

The day did not go well. He moved about in a daze of anxiety, quite certain Jenny would report his behaviour to his mother and he would suffer the humiliating experience of having to explain himself. He considered it might be best for him to find an excuse to cut short his leave and beetle off back to Beeston.

His reticence prompted his mother to say, "Is something the matter, Peter?"

"No, mother, " he lied. "Perhaps I'm relieved to be home and away from it all. Things do get a bit hectic at times, you know."

She moved to him and put her hands on his. "Of course they do, my dear. How are you night landings coming along? You know the ones you wrote to me about when you were training."

He looked around to check they were not being overheard. "Between you and me they are as bad as they ever were. But by the grace of God my co-pilot,

Jaque Bosanquet, sorts me out without fuss, without a need for compliments and without letting on to the rest of the crew. He really is a brick. I'm very lucky, mother, because none of the other crews at Beeston has a second pilot."

She patted his hand. "Do you remember some years ago when I confessed to you about your origins. I told you that Horace was not your father and that I actually conceived you during an overnight fling with a young flying corps officer who I knew from my youth and who went off to war…"

"Yes I do remember, mother. He married another local girl, so you told me, and that he went off to Canada."

"That's right. Well, from my connections in Oxford I heard he had returned to this country and rejoined the air force just before the war started. I contacted him confidentially and told him about your night landing troubles, and asked him to help you in any way he could. I think that's why you have an experienced pilot flying with you."

HC wished she hadn't told him; he felt even more embarrassed about his night landings. He sincerely hoped nobody else got to know of his mother's involvement; it would really make him look very silly, and unable to fend for himself. By now his pride was severely dented. First the rejection by Jenny, and now this disclosure by his mother that she had gone behind his back to try and protect his flying reputation. He felt totally deflated.

When the daylight began to fade that afternoon he spotted Jenny walking across the yard towards the house. Even though a confrontation with her loomed he took every part of her in: her headscarf, her bib and brace overalls which were tucked in Wellington boots and her glowing cheeks painted by the open fresh air of her work. He recalled the brief taste of her sweet moist lips and the glancing view of her warm, firm breasts. God! His thoughts flared. Why do you give them such a slender waist, curving, alluring thighs and rounded bottoms that drive a man crazy with lust and an unquenchable desire to sew the seeds of life?

Dinner was a tense, sombre event that evening. And as soon as it was reasonably possible he made an excuse to leave the table early and take the dogs for a walk.

He walked slowly behind the dogs in the darkness fighting to rationalise his thoughts and anxieties, and debating on whether he should bring the whole thing out into the open, confess to mother and Horace what he had done, and offer his apologies to Jenny.

After a time he sensed, rather than saw, he was being followed. The dogs confirmed this by constantly stopping and looking to the rear. The fact they did not bark indicated they knew who it was. He was half a mile from the house when he halted in a pause of the hedgerows next to a five-barred gate. A figure drew level with the gateway. "Peter! I must speak to you." Jenny called out in the darkness.

She walked in off the lane and approached him. "I want to apologise for what happened this morning," she said, " I should have known better than to come into your room wearing a flimsy night dress and a loose-fitting dressing gown."

He stood looking at her for some time in stunned silence; he could not believe what he was hearing.

"You do understand what I'm saying. Don't you Peter?"

"So you have not reported me to my mother or Horace?"

"Of course not. It never entered my head. I think I'm old enough to deal with this on my own."

He took her hands in his and thanked her. "I know I might have been a bit premature in what I did this morning and that I have only known you for a few hours. But the truth is I am very fond of you, Jenny." He squeezed her hands. "In the past many people have regarded me as indecisive and hesitant. And they were probably right. Yet, at this moment in time, I am very certain about one point – I would like you to marry me."

Croker stood, stripped to the waist, before a mirror rubbing Brylcreem into his head of dark hair. Maurice Clarke sat on the edge of a nearby bed polishing his shoes. "And who is the lucky girl tonight?" he said.

Croker said: "A girl from the parachute section. The one with tight curly hair and cracking blue eyes."

"Not the deadly serious one?" Maurice laughed.

"That's the one."

"Crikey! She'll put you in your place quicker than lightning."

Croker wiped his hands on a towel. "She'll be no different to all the others once she's seen what I got too offer."

"I wouldn't be so sure, Cassanova."

Croker ignored him and stood back to admire himself in the mirror. He liked what he saw and stroked his bootlace thin moustache; he never failed to charm and seduce his lady friends and being an air gunner helped him even more, he told himself. He put on a vest and shirt and tucked them in his trousers and started to put on collar and tie with the use of front and rear studs.

Clarke said: "I bet she don't give you any."

Croker secured his tie and slipped into his tunic. "You want to remember young Maurice you might be dead before you sample a bit of crumpet."

"Who said I want a girl. I'm quite happy with my guns and the air force."

"Stop waffling, " Croker retorted. "And tell me how I look."

"Dressed to kill, you beast." Clarke chortled. "But you won't score with this one tonight."

Croker crossed to the door, paused, looked over his shoulder and laughed, "If I'm not back by midnight you'd better send out a search party."

"It won't be necessary." Clarke scorned. "You'll be back before then with your tail between your legs." and he threw a sock at him to hasten his departure.

He resumed the job of polishing his shoes, dabbing at water in the lid of the boot polish tin with a cloth then rotating it in small circles on the toe cap that had already been smeared with polish. Slowly, progressively, the dull finish rose up bright and polished as ebony.

It reminded him of his early days in the air force when he marched around all day, and polished his boots and buttons by night and was told his destiny was in the cookhouse. But a sudden and urgent demand for air gunners had put out a call for volunteers. The selection board ignored what school he went to or even what work he did before he joined up.

Within a matter of days he was in the thick of a hurried training programme, fighting to understand the bits and pieces of various guns, and learning all the theory attached to sighting. They had so little time they had to learn most of the information parrot-fashion. Everything was so hectic he did not do well in the firing teachers on the ground, and was equally unsuccessful in the air to air gunnery exercises.

Somehow he scraped through the course, was told to sew an air-gunners' brevet on the left chest of his tunic and was told bluntly his survival, and that of the crew he flew with, would depend very much on what he had leant from his mistakes during his training.

Then, as if that was not enough, he was sent on a wireless operator's course which baffled and perplexed him to an even greater extent. How the radio worked challenged his slow intellect and understanding, whilst sending and receiving Morse signals were something of a nightmare. The encouragement by the instructors, the enthusiasm of the other lads on the course and a good helping of providence got him through. He got above average marks, given two stripes to sew on his uniform and told to report to an operational squadron after 92 hours leave.

Providence was also kind when he ended up in HC's crew, because it was Bosey who saw through the gunner's inadequacies and lack of confidence. He got Maurice to spend his spare time picking the brains of the armourers, and the bods in the radio section so as to fill up the gaps in his knowledge regarding the guns and radio.

Thanks to Bosey's advice he now knew exactly where everything was in the glass domain of the upper turret and how it worked. He had a good idea as to how each German aircraft should look through the ring sight. He knew, without hesitating, the causes and remedies should the guns jam in action.

Time in the radio section gave him an opportunity to study in more detail how a radio worked. In his room he had a Morse key which he practiced on for 10 minutes a day. And the w/t section allowed him to listen in to build up his deciphering speed.

The skipper had put him forward for a third stripe that would take him up to the rank of sergeant. That would be good news for his mum and dad.

Having shone his shoes to perfection he took a pair of trousers to an ironing board and sharpened up the creases by using soap, a damp cloth and a hot iron. He was going home and wanted to look the part. He thought his mum was proud of what he had achieved and that their terraced council house would be given a lift by the fact our Maurice mixed and flew with men of the officer class.

He found his thoughts directed to a group photograph over his bed. It reminded him he was one of the lucky ones to have survived this long. Of the 24 young men in the photograph and with whom he had trained as air gunners there was only him and 3 others left. He had placed an ink halo above the head of each one that had fallen in the cause of battle, the news of which he had received through the military grapevine.

Some had gone down over the melting holocaust of a German target ravaged by fire. Others had found a watery grave in the North Sea. A meagre few were prisoners of war.

He spent time polishing the brass buttons on his tunic and great coat. Followed it up with a strip down wash and lay down on the bed. He plunged the room into darkness and lay thinking again about how lucky he was to be with such a brilliant pilot as Bosey. There was nothing Bosey couldn't do to get them out of trouble and Fenny stopped them from getting lost. He drifted into sleep thinking that the war was far from a disaster for him, personally. On reflection he had only gone from strength to strength since he joined the air force.

The station dance was in full swing when Croker arrived. Loud, lively music of a twelve-piece dance band dominated the scene, motivating the mood of the gyrating couples circling the floor like a flock of starlings waiting to migrate. Perfume, beer and cigarette smoke filled the air. He fought his way to the bar and ordered a beer and chaser. He downed them in quick succession and made his way back into the crowd searching for her.

When he did spot her she was already dancing. It appeared she was in great demand. It was a good fifteen minutes before he got a chance to dive in and grab her. The music fell to the tempo of a slow waltz. He held her close with the intention of not letting her escape too easily to somebody else. He had had his eye on her for some weeks when collecting his 'chute and Mae West before going on a raid. She was a bit serious, as Maurice said, but he liked the way she pouted her lips. He was willing to bet that she was a great kisser.

A few days back he had gone into the Safety section on the pretence of asking for some gen on survival packs and chose to go in a quiet time in the hope of talking to her alone. She gave him a leaflet on the information he requested and he feinted a period of study before returning it with his thanks and adding, "Are you going to the station dance on Friday?"

She concentrated on running her fingers along the rigging lines of a parachute. "I have been considering it."

"Any chance of saving a dance for me?"

She paused momentarily in her work and glanced at him. "There is every chance," she said rather haughtily. "If you ask me nicely."

Two nights later he saw her again before they set out for the raid on Cologne. She made him sign for his gear, honoured him with a rare smile, and in a quiet voice told him to take care and wished him lots of luck. Words that turned over and over in his mind during the long, cold flight to, and back from, the target, and which provided him with a strong source of comfort sat on the lonely perch of the rear turret. For the very first time on a raid he experienced no fear. He saw everything around him happen as though he were a bystander. He saw the world rocking and crashing to the exploding, crumping shells and the jabbing searchlights. He spotted winged shapes, crippled, staggering burning forms, slowing down and dropping earthwards. Others disappeared in a distinctive ball of orange flame that scarred the night sky for several seconds.

He saw a machine over the target with two engines on fire. And still beads of flak came up at it until it appeared to roll over and drop out of sight into the conflagration of fires below.

It was the best op he had ever done. The time passed quickly, he didn't feel cold, and for most of the time he floated along with the parting words of the WAAF ringing gently in his ears.

The dance ended. "Like another?" he said desperate to hang on to her.

"Later, perhaps." she smiled

And it was much later. Another hour, in fact, passed before he could get his hands on her, by which time he was fretting at the bit. He did not intend to let her get away this time.

When they finished the next dance he held her hand and led her to the bar. She chose an orange squash and he led her through the jostling bodies out of the hall on to a patio where other couples stood chatting, smoking or huddled in an embrace. He tactfully led her into the shadows around a corner of the building.

"Has anyone told you how pretty you are." he started.

"Many times. It gets very boring."

" Well – I mean what I say."

"Do you?"

"Of course I do. It meant a lot to me what you said the other night before we set out for Cologne. You know, take care and good luck, and all that. I kept thinking about you all the time and never got a chance to feel nervy like I usually do."

She said softly, "I think all of you are very brave."

He waited for her to finish her drink. Then after putting their glasses on a nearby window sill he embraced her, and stole a kiss. Her response came over as cold, inert. He may just as well have been grappling with a bag of potatoes. He tried caressing her and as he did so she took control of his hands when they sought to venture inside her air force shirt or beneath the hem of her skirt. In another attempt to lure her to him he undid the buttons of his trousers and guided her hand upon him. In the darkness he sensed rather than saw the movement. Then he was reeling from a resounding slap across the face.

"How dare you!" she slammed him angrily and hurriedly left.

"Your father wasn't by any chance a donkey," the young woman said.

"What makes you say that?" Maurice Clarke laughed, self-consciously. It was the first time he'd seen a fully naked woman.

"You're very well built and got such stamina." She said. You'd put a lot of men to shame,"

"Good!" he grabbed her. "Let's do it again,"

Her small wiry arms pushed him away, "Oh no you don't. I need a rest, a fag, and a cup of char."

He had picked her up at a dance in the town on the second night of his leave: a pretty little thing who carried an old head on a young body. And what a body it was. He noticed it when she gave him the eye, and for the rest of the evening it had taunted and aroused him to a point he could not refuse her invitation for him to walk her home which turned out to be in a poorer area of the town.

"Cover that monstrous thing up." she jibed, and threw the bedclothes over him.

She stood with her back to him whilst waiting for the kettle to boil. His eyes roamed up and down her nakedness, her sloping shoulders, the way the body tapered to the waist, then flowed out and around her hips and fell away to her shapely legs.

She made the tea and whilst it brewed she turned and smiled down at him.

"How old are you Maurice?"

"Old enough. How old are you?"

"Have a guess."

"About twenty five.

"Blimey! Do I look that old?"

"Twenty five is not old. You're still a Spring chicken."

"Was this your first time?"

"Yes. You took away my virginity, you naughty girl. But I enjoyed every moment of it. Did I do it right?"

She reached down and touched his arm, and smiled sympathetically, " You need to get hold of a nice, clean girl, Maurice. You'd make a good husband and father."

"I'll never forget tonight," he said. "You've been very good to me."

She blushed at his compliment and turned away to pour the tea. Maurice looked around the room, noting the poor circumstances in which she lived. The space was not much bigger than a box room in which a wash basin, a greasy cooker, wardrobe and table were crammed around the bed. A damp patch was visible on the ceiling above the wardrobe and pieces of plaster were flaking off the wall behind the cooker. And the only thing to lend a crumb of comfort to the room was the soft red glow of a table lamp.

The girl turned and handed him a mug of tea, slipped into a dressing gown, lighted two cigarettes, gave him one and slid into the bed beside him. Overhead and on the other side of the ceiling they heard the scurrying, scratching noises of mice.

"Rather them than Jerry bombers." Maurice laughed.

She sidled closer to him and he put an arm around her.

"What's it really like on the raids, Maurice?"

"There's always a bit of excitement when we're over the target and Jerry is throwing up anything he can get hold of – dustbin lids and kitchen sinks. And everybody is a bit on edge when the Jerry night fighters are creeping about. But for much of the time it's dull, boring darkness and, without fail, bloody cold."

She squeezed his arm, "I think you are ever so brave."

He turned to her, "What do you do for a job, Marlene?"

She frowned at him, "You mean you don't know what I do for a living?"

"Well no – you've never told me."

"What did you do before the war, Maurice?"

"I lived at home and worked in a local Ironmongers."

"Did you ever go out on the town with the boys?"

"Not really. We spent our time at the local pub playing darts and dominoes. And I did a bit of exploring on my bike."

"Didn't you ever have a girlfriend?"

"They didn't interest me that much. They giggled too much."

She hesitated before she said, "I'm a tart, Maurice."

He turned suddenly, "A what!"

"A tart – a street girl – a prostitute."

He looked at her, his head on one side and a frown masking his face.

"You know what a prostitute is, don't you?"

"I can't say that I do. I've never heard of the word before."

"A prostitute is a woman who does favours for men and she is paid for it. You know the way I let you sew your wild oats, and let you play with me."

The frown did not leave his face. "You're saying that because you were friendly to me I have to pay you for it. Is that right?"

"In a way, yes."

"But you said I did it right and did it better than other men. I should get a discount."

She reached across and kissed him. He was so young, naïve and strong in a tender sort of way. "You've been such good company I won't ask for any money." She untied her dressing gown. "Come, " she said. "Once more, then you must leave before my landlord knows I've had visitors."

Just after noon the following day he was drinking with his father in the George & Dragon feeling something of a celebrity as people eyed his uniform and his air gunner's single wing brevet. A couple of lads he'd gone to school with had a brief chat. A couple of girls gave him an admiring look. He was also still bathed in the memories of the time he had spent with Marlene. She kept on popping in and out of his thoughts reminding him of her shapely nakedness and the warm and exciting manner in which she had entertained him. The whole episode had added to his pride. He reckoned the experience had made him into a man.

Wilf Walters came from a family of schoolteachers. His mother and father taught in Wales, as did two older brothers. He broke with tradition and joined the Royal

Air Force and trained as an observer in 1936 and later re-mustered to bombaimer just after war on Germany was declared. He quite enjoyed being at Beeston. There wasn't much else he could do to improve his lot on the flying side of things. He enjoyed helping with the navigation and he did his best to plant the bombs accurately on a target, fighting down his concern at the taunting searchlights, the curving beads of flak and the devastating shell bursts, which was, for him, the climax of every operation. It demanded a steady nerve and a great helping of courage. And so far he had been able to meet the demands of the job.

As far as the rest of the crew was concerned he admired Bosey and felt sorry for HC's inadequacies with his night landings. The lad had a nice way about him and was very polite. He didn't consider him a snob as Davey Croker did. But then Davey's restricted childhood had made him ignorant of the fact that there was another life outside of Liverpool. If he but knew, it was Davey who was the snob, of the inverted variety.

Fenny was a good, reliable navigator who was very much on the ball. Wilf shared his swift and positive decisions and judgement. Wilf also got on all right with Edwards, the flight engineer and Sparks the wireless operator. Although he had more to do with them, conversationally, when they rubbed shoulders in the Sergeants' Mess.

And then there was young Maurice Clarke, young and very enthusiastic about his work. Wilf was tempted to father him a bit because the boy was the youngest in the crew and was keen to learn.

Outside of flying and the crew Wilf was rather partial to a weekly game of poker and snooker and a hike into the countryside surrounding the aerodrome. The latter was designed to maintain his physical fitness. He had played rugby regularly up to the start of the war.

It was during one of his hikes he met Majorie Towers who, he was to discover, came from a military family and also married into one. Her Brigadier husband was currently serving somewhere in the Far East. They had been married some twenty years and in that time had only spent about five years living together as man and wife. It did not worry her unduly because she had seen her own mother and father, as a military family, live in similar circumstances.

She held the position of Head Mistress at Beeston village junior school. At forty years of age she was regarded as being in her middle years. She dressed in rather old-fashioned clothes and tied her hair back from a somewhat severe face. She used a bicycle for transport and was frequently seen pedalling through the village, back straight; head held high, a stern expression on her face. She never mixed with the villagers and you could count the number of her friends on one hand. Most of the villagers thought her rather aloof and claimed she behaved rather like an old maid. Her school colleagues thought she showed all the traits of a spinster

Wilf met her of an evening when he was doing his weekly hike and Majorie was walking her small Yorkshire Terrier, a dog that did not take kindly to anyone getting too close to its owner. It had a habit of slinking up on Wilf from behind and taking a dive at his ankles. Fortunately he used his air force pattern ankle boots for his hikes and their thick leather spared him from injury. But he was determined the dog should refrain from its infuriating habit. He chose a moment when he thought the dog was racing for his ankles. As it accelerated forward Wilf swung the heel of his boot rearwards. It had the effect of a sharp collision and as the dog clamped its teeth, instead of sinking into the ankle of the boot, the top row of teeth drove into the solid heel and the bottom row cracked and grated on the metal tip nailed to the heel. There was wild yelp as the animal lifted into the air, turned head over heels, and came back to earth, laying on its side, tongue hanging out, looking rather sorry for itself.

Wilf thought Majorie would be annoyed. Instead she said, "You won't do that again in a hurry, will you Brigadier." Wilf thought it most amusing that she labelled the dog with the rank of her absent soldier husband.

Majorie was quite smitten by the young, energetic airman and after their third meeting she invited him into her country cottage home. She put water and biscuits down for the dog. But it ignored her and retired sulkily to its basket.

"Would you care for tea, Mr Walters?"

"Thank you," he smiled at her. "But please call me Wilf. Don't let's be so formal,"

His rich, baritone, Welsh voice appealed to her. And the fact he came from a family that shared her profession of teaching, made her think they had much in common.

"Excuse me saying," she said. "But I have a strange habit of putting my choice of name to a person. You don't look a bit like a Wilfred to me."

"Really?" he laughed deeply. "Then tell me, what would you call me?"

She moved to him and held his strong, capable hands, "You promise not to be offended?"

He nodded and held her with his twinkling brown eyes.

She paused before she said, " I would rather like to call you Teddy."

He threw his head back and roared with laughter.

"Don't you approve?" she said.

He said, "I don't think they'd like it in Wales. But the rest of the crew might find it amusing. Flight Sergeant 'Teddy' Walters indeed. It has quite a nice ring about it doesn't it?"

The evening turned into something special for her in that for the first time in an age she had male company in her home. Over cups of tea Teddy helped her finish the crossword in the Daily Telegraph. Then they sat listening to classical music on the radio for a couple of hours and she rather liked it when he took her hand and held it. A glow rose up within her, and she felt a new impetus flowing into her lonely world.

As the daylight faded at the windows, so her thoughts and feelings drifted further away from her responsibilities as a head mistress and a wife. And when Teddy pulled her head onto his shoulder and put an arm around her, she kicked her shoes off and drew her feet up on to the settee and closed her eyes as she sought to reclaim her lost youth.

Later she felt an urge to fuss over him a bit. She made him a supper, a Welsh Rarebit no less. She made mugs of cocoa to go with it and they dined in the solitary light of a yellow shaded table lamp, close and totally happy, their hearts and minds bound up in the amorous, stirring overtures of the string orchestra.

At eleven o'clock he said it was time for him to leave.

"Do you have to?" she whispered.

"I don't have a late night pass, you see. And I wouldn't like you to become the victim of local gossip because neighbours noticed you had a strange man staying overnight."

She didn't tell him that the nearest house to her was half a mile away and that she had never engaged in social intercourse with the occupants.

"You will come again, Teddy, won't you?" she said at the door

He took her in his arms and in the deep Welsh voice that made her cringe and go weak at the knees he said, "Your order is my command, my lady."

Walters made his next visit to her when Bosey got them off on four days leave. He made his way across fields of wheat and rye, adjacent to the aerodrome, and down through a bridle path beyond. In the darkness of the evening he thought he heard crickets chirping and felt certain he saw the dark shape of a hedgehog shuffling across the road. Down to his right in a roadside ditch something scurried and rustled the dried, brown, fallen leaves left over from last autumn. Overhead the stars brought an extravagance to the sky with their sparkling gems that were strung out on the deep blue cushion of the night. He felt happy and proud to recall he was over half way through his tour of operations and was now considered to be something of a veteran. But he did not take it for granted. Since his time with the squadron they had replaced fifty percent of the aircraft and crews that had gone down on a raid. And the losses continued to mount at an unhealthy rate.

He reached the front gate and, carried by a wave of lightheartedness, he vaulted over it. He paused to straighten his tunic and remove his forage cap. In anticipation of what the dog would do, and before he rapped the knocker, he stood with a boot standing on its heel and with the full area of the sole facing the spot of the door opening, through which he thought the dog would bolt. And sure enough it did so as soon as he used the knocker and Majorie opened the door. In a space of about eight inches it forced its way through and went at full pelt into the studded sole of the military boot. The force of the impact sent it leaping into the air. It came down nose first sprawling and yelping. The airman, as a further warning, lifted his boot and slammed it on the ground. The dog sped to its basket and lay in it whimpering at its mistress with appeals for help.

Majorie simply said, "You ought to know Teddy by now, Brigadier."

She turned to the visitor and before he could hand her a box of chocolates and a small bouquet of flowers she was all over him, "Where have you been, Teddy?" She feverishly embraced him. "It's nearly three weeks since I've seen you."

"The Jerries have kept us busy," he said breathlessly. "We are at war you know."

"Yes – yes, I know that. But you could have sent me a card or a note just to let me know you were well. There was a big crash over at Posely Bridge last week and a smaller one the week before. I couldn't help thinking the worse."

The first crash had been a Halifax, returning from a raid during which it had taken a pasting from ground fire. It had lost two engines. Managed to get the undercarriage down for landing but not the flaps. It came in at excessive speed, the wheels collapsed and it skidded past the over-run of the runway through a hedgerow, across a country lane, through another hedgerow, into a ploughed field, taking two telephone poles and the connecting wires with it. There was no fire and all the crew survived.

The second prang was both dramatic and fatal. The Halifax was taking off, at night, fully loaded with fuel, and its complement of bombs. At a critical time when speed is fighting to overcome weight, and bring lift to the wings, an engine or possibly two lost their revs. Walters could well imagine the pilot's ordeal of fighting to orientate himself in the darkness of the night. What is the speed? The Halifax is turning! But which way? Check the ball in the turn and slip. It's out to the left. Kick on left rudder! She's coming round. But the speed is still falling away; in no way will she fly and the last couple of lights of the flarepath are approaching. " Captain to crew. We're not going to make it. Brace yourselves!" Close the throttles. Collapse the undercarriage. Fuel OFF! Ignition OFF! Electrics OFF! The grating of heavy metal and the bomb doors in the belly of the fuselage screeched along the concrete runway and then changed to a lurching, bumping, thumping journey as the Halifax made its exit from the aerodrome through the boundary fences, its weight giving it the momentum of a battering ram. It crashed through a small wood. The fuel ignited and this quickly spread to the bomb bays. Just before it came to a halt in the middle of a ploughed field the whole lot erupted in a sheet of flame. Nobody survived the ensuing inferno.

Engulfed by a storm of passion Majorie pushed him into a chair and relieved him of his boot, socks, shirt, trousers, underpants and vest.

"Control yourself, madam!" he mocked her.

"Don't tease me Teddy." She hurried his naked form to the bedroom, shut the door, and flicked the key in the lock and, in full view of her husband's photograph on the bedside table, she ripped open her lace-trimmed blouse and a button flew through the air to land upon her dressing table. He froze in admiration of her large, noble breasts. How they cried out to be touched, to be caressed. Majorie removed her skirt and underwear.

"You mustn't neglect me for so long, Teddy." She fell backwards onto the bed, pulling him with her, quite oblivious to the weight of his hairy, muscular body. She wrapped her arms about him and set her legs akimbo.

He hesitated, knowing he had forgotten something.

"Please, Teddy. Don't delay it any longer," she pleaded.

"Hang on a moment." He wrestled to escape her crushing hold on him.

"What for? What for? Teddy?" she cried out.

"I haven't taken the precautions."

She reached up and pulled him back down on her. "Don't worry about that tonight. I'm quite safe."

And young and inexperienced as he was, he believed her.

Five

Within days of returning from their leave they were back on operations in earnest. Clarke's encounter with Marlene and what he had experienced with her continued to flit in and out of his memory. He enjoyed the view of her nakedness. He could feel the smoothness and warmth of her skin to his touch and how she touched and stroked him in return. The impact she had on him was so great he could feel her breasts and loins pressing against him beneath his heavy flying gear as the Halifax wheeled away from the target. It was Essen again with 800 hundred aircraft taking part. The moon was up and they had somehow managed to get through an intense barrage of ack-ack, flak and batteries of searchlights. Whilst around, above, and beneath them the air shook to the booms and crumps, the shrieks, the whistling, the streams of light, flashes of light and spasmodic sheets of light.

"Keep your eyes peeled gunners." The skipper called. " I've already seen two Jerry night fighters. They'll probably pounce once we clear the target."

Maurice kept his turret revolving whilst at the same time he rubbed at his groin. In the last couple of minutes he had developed an irritating itch in the area of his crutch. And his thick gloves and heavy flying clothing prevented him from having a good scratch.

It steadily got worse; it was if a bee had got into his underpants. He'd had nothing like it before. A shadow darted through the sight of his revolving gun. He paused, and strained his eyes to determine what it was. And he was on the verge of thinking that the night was playing tricks with his imagination when a large explosion and blinding light lit up the starboard wing and the engines over which he was looking.

"What the hell was that?" somebody called.

"I think it was another Halifax." Maurice said and vigorously rubbed at his groin. If it went on much longer it would drive him bonkers.

HC said, "We'd better start jinking. I'd be ashamed if that happened to us."

In a sudden surge of moonlight Maurice saw a dark winged shape bank steeply

onto their tail. Before he could call, Dave Croker let rip from the rear turret.

"Keep jinking, skipper. We got an unfriendly visitor on our tail."

Maurice waited for his chance; if he fired now he would more than likely shoot the Halifax tail off.

"He's gone underneath!" Croker shouted.

"There he is." Bosey called. "Starboard side, young Maurice. Be ready as the skipper corkscrews"

Maurice hesitated too long; he was frightened he might hit the starboard wing and engines of the Halifax, and the itching was not going away. The night fighter disappeared, unharmed, into the night.

They flew on for a time without being molested. But there were a couple of distant booms and flashes that indicated two of their number had not escaped the menacing night fighters.

Maurice grew desperate with the unrelenting itching. Somehow or other he had to get at the bareness of his groin. It would mean asking the skipper to let him leave the turret, and it would mean descending to warmer air where he could remove his gloves and open up the fly of his trousers. Worst of all he'd have to explain why. He had until they made their landfall on the Dutch coast to come up with an explanation. That would be the earliest time he could expect the skipper to drop lower. He pondered and scratched.

Meanwhile in the rear turret Croker sat staring morosely at the moon. It didn't worry him that he hadn't got the Jerry night fighter; it didn't register that the fighter might very well have done them serious damage; he couldn't give a damn anymore. He was so engrossed with his thoughts he did not see other Halifax bombers following up in the rear as dark shapes, which occasionally shattered the face of the moon. He scarcely heard the noise of the engines such was his lack of concentration.

The truth was that his pride had taken a severe denting; a woman had not shot him down before. He had been unable to face her when collecting his gear for the raid. He blushed from ear to ear with embarrassment, signed the chit, and got out as fast as he could. He had thought of slipping her a note of apology but then he thought she'd think even less of him when she saw his atrocious writing and spelling.

What shattered him most of all was the fact he genuinely liked her; he thought she had a bit of class and he might learn something about how the other half of society lived. She dressed smartly, wore her auburn hair neatly as a roll on the back of her head and she wore no make-up or nail varnish. She had big, bright eyes and her face glowed with colour. And – yes – she did have a shapely body…

"Everything all right back there, rear gun?" HC's voice broke into his thoughts.

" Well – um – er. All okay, skipper." he stirred.

"Keep guard for a spell. I've released the top gun who is dying for a pee."

Edwards the flight engineer said: "Want me to take his place in the turret skipper?"

"Thanks engines. I think we're okay. He won't be long."

Edwards shrugged and thought, don't think I never offered. He ran his eyes over the fuel contents gauges and noted the position of the fuel cocks. It wasn't unknown for a stray piece of shell to hit a tank during the hell and commotion of the run up to the target when everybody were too busy to notice and the next thing anyone knew the fuel was draining away into the night sky.

Everything, however, was as it should be and in the smooth flight of the Halifax and the steady beat of the engines his thoughts began to drift. He looked at his watch; this time last night he was with Joyce: the widow of another flight engineer who went down on a raid on Berlin two months back. He and her husband Bernie had been great friends and following his death Edwards had provided her with, as best he could, solace and a shoulder to cry on.

But last night that all changed. They went to the local 'hop' in the Beeston village hall as they had done a number of times before. And then some two hours before the dancing and partying was due to end Joyce asked him if they could leave early.

Usually he walked her to the gate of her front garden, exchanged farewell with a brief kiss, and he walked back to the aerodrome. This time she stopped and took both his hands in hers, "Would you like to come in for a nightcap, Ken?"

He looked down at her, "Are you sure it won't start tongues wagging about it being too soon after Bernie getting the chop?"

"I'm not really concerned about my neighbours, Ken. I feel awful sending you off each time after you have given me a good evening out. And there is something else – I think the time has come for you and me to stop pretending."

"Pretending?"

"Yes. Pretending we are just respectable good friends when in fact we have more than a passing fancy for each other." She played with the collar of his coat. "It's true, isn't it?"

In the absence of an answer she unlocked the door of her home and led him inside. She put more coal on the fire and got him seated before the hearth whilst she went off to prepare mugs of cocoa.

As he looked into the flickering flames he thought of the times when he was at home with his mum and dad and brother and sisters on Saturday evenings, and his dad baked chestnuts and potatoes in the fire. He remembered splitting the spuds open and putting butter salt and pepper on the fleshy insides. The mere thought of it made his mouth water. Home, sweet home, he smiled. And it reminded him that it was time he sent a letter to his mum and dad.

Joyce came into the room carrying the mugs of cocoa on a tray. She sat on a rug before the hearth, using the front of the settee as a backrest and invited him to join her.

"Engines?" HC broke into his trail of memories.

"Yes, skipper."

"Nip aft and see what top gun is up to. He's been gone ten minutes or more. And I can't get him on the radio."

As the engineer made to get out of his seat Maurice announced, "Top gun back in position, skipper."

"Thank you, top gun."

Bosey smiled to himself in the darkness. He was both pleased and amused at how much HC had change since coming back from leave. Overnight he had changed from a timid, hesitant boy into a mature officer, who moved with a sense of purpose, spoke with a positive tone in his voice and who could make swift accurate decisions. Bosey speculated on what had caused the sudden change of character. And came to the conclusion that, perhaps, the clue lay in the surprise announcement that he was getting married.

He had led the flight that night exactly as a captain should, no hesitating, no fudging and just the right note of authority in his voice. There only remained the night landing back at Beeston.

They plodded on through the night dodging around the bulbous fringes of a restless, filling cumulus. HC passed the course changes he made to Fenny who plotted them on his Mercators chart.

Clarke continued wincing and rubbing at his groin. Croker thought seriously how he might work his ticket to get off flying and away from Beeston. And, more importantly, away from the woman who had seriously wounded his pride.

Edwards's thoughts drifted off again to Joyce and how the night had ended up with them stripping naked and making love on the carpet, in the flickering light and heat from the small hearth fire. She had a voracious appetite.

Sparks got a couple of radio fixes and gave them to Fenny who compared them to his DR position. They were half way across the North Sea. Another hour and a bit and they'd be having buns and cocoa at the debriefing. God Willing!

Wilf Walters could not stop his thoughts drifting off to Marjorie. Her Teddy, indeed! But what he could not get out of his mind was what she hid beneath the frumpy old-fashioned clothes she wore. Dressed – she looked old, cold, serious, aloof. In the nude she transformed herself into something youthful, quite delightful and highly desirable. The vanilla colour of her skin rose and fell gently upon her contours, ascending to the summits of her prominent breasts, converging and diverging from her waist and sweeping round her thighs. She submitted herself to him with the grace and eloquence of a young goddess with the undulating and rhythmical movements of her body. She gratified him, in full, in a way that only a woman of her hunger could.

In the noisy drum of the Halifax nose cone he had to will himself to get his thoughts back on the job. He had spotted a white tide mark etching the East Coast of dear old England. He reported it to Fenny.

Half an hour later they arrived at Beeston. They were in the circuit on the downwind leg; all landing checks complete, when a Halifax collided with another on the runway causing mayhem. They learnt later that the first one collapsed on its belly shortly after it touched down and instead of slithering to the end of the runway it spun around and stopped about three quarters of the way along the runway. The second Halifax received a red signal from the control van, telling him to abandon the approach and go round again. But the Halifax was below decision height. The captain elected to continue the landing and when he got on the ground he could see he was moving too fast to avoid hitting the other aircraft. He retracted his undercarriage but rather than slowing him down, as he had anticipated, the grinding, spark-showering Halifax ploughed into the other doomed bomber.

HC and all the other Beeston machines were diverted to Coleyfield thirty miles down the coast. Croker cursed the inconvenience. It had put paid to his decision to report sick at the end of the operation. And poor, young Maurice Clarke was still itching like mad.

Bosey grinned with satisfaction. HC dealt competently with the sudden change of plan. He got the engines up to power, got the undercarriage and flaps up, and swung up in a climbing turn on to the QDM for Coleyfield, given by Beeston. He then changed the radio to the Coleyfield frequency. He concluded by alerting the crew to remain vigilant. They could expect bit of a circus at their destination.

Not once during the entire operation had HC sought Bosey's assistance. And likewise Bosey had not found it necessary to intervene. Even joining the busy queue for landing at Coleyfield HC had it nicely under control, keeping the Halifax poised on a balance of flap and power and an adequate distance from the machine in front. He swung gently onto the final approach, "Captain to crew. Prepare for landing. " He said boldly.

There was none of the usual comments from Corker or Walters.

They floated towards the flarepath at reduced power, full flap, at the correct speed and with, perhaps, all of them feeling, from time to time, the heavy bomber swaying and lurching beneath their seats, as it sank down over the hidden countryside and its inhabitants. As they approached the threshold lights HC brought the speed back another five knots. And as the second of the runway lights swept by he slowly closed the throttles. They fell to earth in a perfect three-point landing.

They slept the night in a gathering of easy chairs in a transit hut and received buns and hot, strong, sweet air force tea served by a clutch of pretty WAAFs. Maurice noticed that Davey Croker paid no attention to them. That was most unusual. As for Maurice himself he had not succeeded in getting rid of his uncomfortable crutch. It felt hot, sticky and sore, and if the itching went on much longer he'd pull his hair out. He spent most of the night in the privacy of a toilet where he could let some air fan the heat and to some extent sooth the soreness and itching.

They flew back to Beeston the next day and saw the remains of the two aircraft, that had collided, had been pushed to the side of the runway. Maurice rather hoped he could talk to Davey Croker about his itching problem when they got back to their quarters in the sergeants' mess. But Davey was in a very dark, angry mood and as soon as they arrived he packed a small kitbag and walked out without saying a word.

Eventually Maurice plucked up the courage and walked to the sick quarters to report his ailment. He was called into a small consulting room by a male orderly dressed in a white jacket and who behaved strangely by talking and gesturing like a woman.

"What can I do for you, my dear?"

Somewhat embarrassed Maurice stammered, "I...I...I've got a lot of itching and soreness." He hesitated.

"Right. You've got a lot of soreness. But where, my dear?" the orderly lisped.

"Down there," Maurice pointed with a finger.

The orderly moved to him and loosened the belt of his trousers. "Now drop them. And your underpants."

Self-consciously Maurice did so, the colour raging in his face. Goodness, gracious he had never felt so embarrassed. The orderly crouched down in front of him with a surgical gloved hand holding a tool shaped like a silver butter knife. "Right! Be a dear and lift your shirt front so I can have a good look." Maurice conformed and stood looking at the ceiling trying to forget what was going on.

The orderly lifted his manhood up with the flat face of the butter knife to look underneath. "Quite a handsome specimen," he remarked. " And beautifully shaped."

Maurice was tempted to tell him to stop all the waffling and get on and tell him what was wrong and what treatment he needed.

"You've been dipping it in dirty water, haven't you?" the orderly said in somewhat of a matronly tone. "If it was a woman on this station, I've got to know. She needs urgent treatment. Otherwise she'll be passing it on to every Tom, Dick and Harry at Beeston"

"What's the dirty water got to do with it?" Maurice snapped.

"Nothing really, my dear. It's just something I use as a polite way of saying you've been with a prostitute."

"So what are you trying to tell me?"

"You've reported it early, my dear. So you'll get away with a good splash of disinfectant and a course of tablets." The orderly walked to a cabinet and washbasin in a corner, stopped halfway, turned and said, "My! You are beautifully hung." He continued to the cabinet, shaking his head and swinging his hips like a woman. He came back presently with a semi-circular enamel bowl containing a white liquid whose smell, mixed with that of ether, characterised all sick bays and hospitals. It brought back memories for Maurice of his visit as a boy to have his tonsils and adenoids removed. The smell signified danger and of being amongst strangers.

The orderly said quietly, "Now, clench your fists and grit your teeth. This is going to hurt a bit."

Maurice threw his head back further and looked directly at the ceiling, trying to pretend it wasn't happening to him. Good God! What a mess I'm in, he thought. I'll never go with a strange woman again. I promise. What a sight he must look with his trousers and underpants girding his ankles and hiding his shoes. And him clutching at his tie and shirt, holding it clear of his loins...I never want to go through this again...

The intensity of the soreness that struck him was if someone was sawing through his vitals. He clenched his fists and barred his teeth to muffle his shrieks of discomfort. It was so severe it made his eyes water.

"Hold on a little longer. I'm nearly finished." The orderly soaked another wad of cotton wool in the disinfectant and dabbed it at the infected area. The tears trickled down the young air gunner's face.

At long last the orderly wrapped the affected organ in a layer of lint and stowed it gently in the gunner's underpants. "I'll leave you to do your trousers," he said.

Maurice wiped the tears of pain from his eyes with the back of a hand, tucked his shirt in his trousers, pulled his braces back up and replaced his tunic.

"Take two in the morning and two just before you go to bed," the orderly said. "These are to chase the infection out from the inside. Don't even look at another girl till you've got rid of this lot. And stay off the beer whilst you're on the tablets." He paused. "Oh! And one more thing before you go." He undid a top pocket of the gunner's tunic and jammed two packets of condoms inside. "Use these in future and you'll avoid getting the clap," He gently patted the gunner's face with both hands, which Maurice found very odd. So much so he blushed. "You're too much of a nice boy to get mixed up with tainted woman," the effeminate orderly looked sympathetically at him. "Now get along and keep clean." And he pouted his lips as if blowing a kiss in farewell. For a man he had rather big lips, Maurice noticed, and his face was smooth and soft and bereft of hair.

Maurice had reached the door and was on the point of turning the handle when the orderly said, "By the way, there is just one more thing."

"Yes?" Maurice said slowly, warily, expecting to be paid another dubious compliment, or, told to abstain from another pleasure in his life.

" What do you know, if anything, about sergeant Croker?"

" Davey and I are in the same crew. I'm top gun and he's rear gun."

" Well, I don't know whether your skipper knows it, or not, but Croker reported in sick today and wants to be put off flying, saying he's fed up bombing women and kids."

Croker lay in the sick bay, at Beeston, looking morosely up at the ceiling when she suddenly appeared at his bedside. At first he couldn't believe it and when he did he felt so ashamed he wished he could have disappeared into thin air "What are you doing here?" he said out the corner of his mouth.

"I might ask the same of you," she said brightly.

"I've had enough. It's as simple as that."

"Enough of what?"

"Flying and bombing women and kids."

"But that's not true, is it?"

He looked askance at her. "Anyway, what's it got to do with you?"

"I had a visit from Flight Sergeant Bosanquet. He and Sergeant Clarke reckon I put you in here."

"They said that?"

"In so many words, yes."

He turned away from her again unable to face her. Two other patients in beds on either side of him were listening and smiling.

The girl stirred and pulled the curtains around his bed. "Is that better?"

He summoned the courage to face her, grateful for the privacy, "Look," he spoke in a loud whisper. "Rightly or wrongly I made a pass at you. And you shot me down. Yes – it hurt and I felt a right idiot. But the truth is I've had enough of bombing women and kids on the raids."

She took his hand and held it. He was acutely aware that her clothed breasts were only a matter of inches from his nose and he could smell the perfumed soap she used.

"But you don't actually kill women and children, do you?"

"What d'you mean?"

"You don't drop the bombs, yourself. And neither do you guide the pilot to the target and press the button that releases the bombs."

"Well, no –but,"

"There's no ifs and buts about it. I'm told that sergeant Walters, the bombaimer in the crew, that's his job."

"Yes, but I'm part of the crew that drops the bombs."

"That's right and you try to shoot down German pilots who have wives and children. Is that not so? And never forget it was the Germans who started this war, bombing women and children in London, Southampton, Plymouth, Coventry and other English cities."

He quickly came to the conclusion that he would never get one over her. She was a good deal brighter than he was and much more mature. He squirmed when he thought of how he had tried to touch her up that night and she slapped his face. He realised now that he had insulted her intelligence and showed too little respect for her as a woman of quality.

"Well – I suppose you are right, in a way." he said.

She fussed around him for a spell, puffing up his pillow, and straightening the bedclothes. She also took a comb off the top of his bedside locker and ran it through his hair. "Now, sergeant Croker, I'll leave you to think on what I've said. I'll come back tomorrow and you can tell me what you have decided. I hope it's going to be, that you are coming to collect your kit for the next operation."

He badly wanted her to stay. He desperately wanted to say something to her but didn't know how to frame it. He grabbed a fold in her skirt and jerked her to a halt as she turned to go. "You promise to come back tomorrow?" he pleaded in a whisper.

She reached down and removed the grip of his hand on her skirt. She placed the hand back beneath the bedclothes, leant over and kissed him on the forehead. One of her covered breasts pressed into the shoulder of his pajama jacket. "I promise," she said quietly, positively. Drew the bed screens apart and vanished.

Six

Wing Commander Timothy Herby studied the casualty list. It made for gloomy reading. The wing, under his command, had lost some fifteen aircraft and crews on the previous night's operation. He tried to stop it getting at him, these losses night after night of so many of the youth of Britain and the Commonwealth nations. But week after week the choking feeling rose higher in his chest. It was not unlike a bout of indigestion.

Now there would be the racing around to get replacement aircraft and personnel from the pools, chasing the aircraft pools and training schools. Then there would be spares needed for the aircraft that came back with battle damage. And organising telegrams to the relatives of the missing crews. Whilst higher up the chain of command there would come orders for the next raid and a call for maximum effort.

Behind him he heard the patter of rain on the tall high window. He turned to see rivulets of water running down the glass squares and beyond the window a totally overcast grey sky with fracto-stratus scurrying along beneath it.

"I think it's the break we've been waiting for," Harry Foswaite, his adjutant said.

Herby got up and crossed to the window. "Have you seen a recent forecast?"

"No. But that lot outside, it's got all the symptoms of a warm front with about four hundred miles of unsettled weather behind it. I don't think group are likely to call a raid for the next two or three nights."

"Let's hope you are right, Harry." Herby returned to his desk. Sergeant Polly Cinders came in and served them mugs of tea. She was Herby's admin assistant, a smart, and efficient secretary with a quiet, voluble tongue and who was in love with her boss. She was waiting for him to make the first move.

"Any messages about the next raid?" Herby said. He was referring to the teleprinter in her office that connected the Wing with Group.

"No, sir. I don't think it likely now. It would be too short notice for tonight."

"Right. I must get on," Foswaite said and left.

Herby handed the casualty list to the girl for filing. "Anything else I should know about?"

"Oh, yes. Squadron leader Mellows and Flight Sergeant Bosanquet are waiting to see you, sir."

For a moment his memory of the two men deserted him. "Any idea why they are here?"

"They said it was something to do with Hadley-Chase."

"Right! Show them in. And could I trouble you to make tea for them."

Mellows and Bosanquet came in smiling through a lurking weariness. They'd been on the previous night's raid. He greeted them cheerfully and thanked them for their time.

Mellows said, "It's Hadley -Chase, sir."

"Not causing you any problems, I hope."

"Not at all. In fact he's told flight sergeant Bosanquet that he thinks it's time he went off on his own with the crew like the rest of the squadron."

"He does, does he?" He turned to Bosanquet. "What are your views, Flight? Is he ready?"

"From his performance last night I'd say he's got it all together, at last. He flew the operation like a veteran. He had to contend with a pile-up on the runway and a diversion to Coleyfield. He carried out a landing at a strange aerodrome, at night, and it was a corker of a three-pointer. I never had to intervene once during the entire operation."

"Really!"

Sergeant Cinders came in and served the tea and retreated.

Bosey said, "He dropped a hint to me and the navigator that he was getting married."

Herby leaned back in his chair looking rather pleased. "Between us three I think his mother is going to be very grateful to you two for organising this. Now – how do you propose we go about it? Send him off straight away, or, send somebody else with him for a second opinion?"

Bosey said, "You might like to check him out for yourself, sir."

" That's a good idea. But we'll have to do it under cover because Group has grounded me for three months. I'll come down to the squadron to get kitted out and have a look round a Halifax. I've not flown one before. How's that?"

"Splendid idea," said Mellows. "I'll arrange it for you, sir."

The next raid was called raid three days later and Herby went down the squadron as soon as the order came through from Group HQ. He got sergeant Bosanquet to put his name on the equipment list. Then had him show him around a Halifax. He had completed two tours of operations on twin engine aircraft, the Whitley and the Wellington. It would be his first trip in a four engine heavy bomber.

Bosey had told HC and Fenny of the wing commander's involvement, following the meeting at Wing HQ. Now, as the rest of the crew arrived, he broke the news and introduced them. Sparks showed no reaction to the fact they'd be flying with a senior officer. Clark, Edwards and Walters acted a little shyly but were rather proud that the wing commander should choose to fly with them. He must think something of their skills, they decided.

Croker, on the other hand, still had reservations about the officer class. He respectfully saluted Herby and told him who he was in the crew. And when the officer told him to carry on he wandered away to his turret looking miserable and tense. He was not reassured that the flying would be safe without Bosey in the crew, and the fact he'd overheard the Winco saying it would be his first flight in a Halifax. Equally he was not certain he had done the right thing by allowing the girl in the parachute section to coax him back to flying.

They were briefed at 2000hrs. And airborne at 2130hrs, leaving a hard frost on the ground to fly up into a bright moon lit sky that made many of them feel vulnerable to night fighters. Other pilots said it gave them a better chance of seeing the fighters. They plodded up to 17,000 feet. Walters reported them crossing the coast to Fenton. And the navigator plotted their position on his Mercators chart, and ran a ground speed check. HC conferred with Edwards as to the state of the engines for the long haul across the North Sea to the target many miles beyond. The engineer gave a good report.

HC contacted the gunners next telling them to check their oxygen supply and they could now test their guns. They all noticed rather oddly that Davey Croker, having been sullen and morose at the briefing and all the way out to the aircraft, now said briskly and efficiently, "Rear gun to captain. Guns tested and all satisfactory."

"Thank you rear gun." HC said with a hint of laughter in his voice.

Croker, perched in his turret, looked out to the rear of the Halifax and watched the moon lighting up the many other pursuing Halifax bombers; dark four engine winged shapes whose Perspex turrets and cockpit windows had occasion to glint in the light of the moon. He removed a wrapper from a toffee with gloved hands and slipped the sweet in behind his oxygen mask into his mouth. He still could not get over what had happened. He hadn't waited for her to come back the next day to the sick bay. He voluntary signed himself off the sick that same day and returned to the Sergeants' mess.

He'd got in the queue to collect his parachute and life jacket for the current raid, feeling nervous at what she might say when she noticed he had returned to flying. Would she mock him? Would she let on to others what had happened in the sick bay and how he had behaved like a wimp?

She did neither. As he drew level with her she placed a parachute and harness on the counter before him and placed on top his yellow life jacket and a torch and spare battery pack. Next she slid a wooden board holding an equipment list toward him with a pencil for him to sign. Under the crocodile clip at the top of the board was a folded piece of paper with his name printed on. As he pushed the board back she stealthily released the paper and slid it towards him, "Have a safe trip," she smiled briefly at him and turned her attention to the next man in the line.

His first chance to read the note never came until they all arrived at the aircraft for the raid and he was settling himself in the rear turret. He unfolded it and in the light of his torch he read:

WELCOME BACK TO FLYING, DAVID.
HOW ABOUT ADRINK IN THE BAT
TOMORROW NIGHT. SAY ABOUT 7.30
FLY WELL AND FLY SAFELY.
BEST REGARDS, FIONA

If he read it once that night, he must have read it twenty times. He had his first taste of being choked by his emotions. He felt a deep happiness and relief that had him shedding tears, which froze on the outside of his oxygen mask. He felt so elated he badly wanted to dance and sing about it. The Bat was a small pub about 4 miles distant from the aerodrome. He'd only used it once and considered it too dark and dingy. The beer there tasted like vinegar. Most of the crews used the Scarlet Woman a more modern and imposing building set amongst the other architecture of the Village Square. But if Fiona wanted the Bat, then the Bat public house it would be. Fiona – what a name? A bit posh perhaps. But it suited her short dark hair and clear blue eyes. Her voice, pitched a little high, pronounced clearly every word she spoke. Her hourglass anatomy in the tailored uniform she wore, he noticed, was not of the thick serge material associated with NCO rank. Her material was that of the officer class and he was curious as to how she got away with it. He was not to know she paid for the uniform herself. He formed the impression she was from a rich, top-drawer family. And he had, as yet, to learn that she actually came from humble parentage who had sacrificed much to pay for her private education, which had given her the necessary poise and confidence to start out on her adult life. She had applied twice for a commission in the air force, having got five certificates of merit at school. She was not deterred by the fact she had been rejected not once but twice.

She was confident that she was as smart, both in appearance and wit, as any of the other women officers she met. She had always suspected it and, now, even more so. The selection boards were not impressed by her family background, a porter father who worked on the railways and a mother who cleaned a junior school for a few hours per week.

"Captain to crew. We're within range of the night fighters. Keep your eyes peeled."

Forty minutes later Fenton calculated they were twenty minutes from the target and Walters, in the nose, confirmed it when he saw tapering cones of light probing the sky some miles ahead amongst which a shell scarred the night air with a brilliant flash of light. As they drew closer they could hear the booming and crumping of the ground defences. Then up came the curving arcs of flak. The Halifax seemed to lurch and sway of its own accord, like a horse bulking at a firework display of jumping jacks.

"Bomb doors open!" Walters called.

"It's all yours, bombs!" HC acknowledged.

It was always a long, tense crawl up to the target with the pilot attempting to keep calm and setting an example to the rest of the crew, and making small corrections on the flying controls as dictated by the bombaimer. The shell bursts got closer, louder and more dazzling. As did the smaller but lethal balls of flak. The night grew lighter as the searchlights grew in number and rallied against the sky. A number of aircraft winged unintentionally into the beams like moths attracted to a candle flame. And like some of the moths, whose wings burned, so bombers had their wings set alight by an accurately placed shell or a seam of flak balls.

"Bombs gone!" shouted Walters. It was if each of the crew breathed a huge sigh of relief at the same time into their facemasks and was heard over the R/T.

"Close bomb doors!" HC called. The wing commander sitting beside him complied.

HC opened the throttles and the corresponding roar of the engines dulled the noise of the ground defences. He was forced to crank the Halifax over hard, down and around a menacing searchlight.

Gradually they pulled away from the target and set the course home on the compass as given by Fenton.

"Captain to crew. Keep your eyes open for fighters. Rear gun. Is everything alright back there."

"Everything is satisfactory, skipper. Thank you."

Maurice Clarke smiled. Our Davey is getting polite all of a sudden, he thought

"Top gun. Everything well with you?"

"All okay, skipper."

After checking the rest of the crew they flew on in the failing light of the moon. It had been almost overhead when they set out. Now its azimuth was about forty degrees. HC allowed the aircraft to fly on the trim and retrieved a flask of coffee from his flight bag and was about to offer the wing commander a drink when Walters called, "I think we're getting bit close to an aircraft ahead of us, skipper." HC replaced the thermos in the bag, took the controls to hand and banked around to the right of the other machine. As they drew level the moonlight showed the other Halifax to be crabbing through the air, crippled, as it was, by the windmilling propeller of a failed engine, smoke streaming from its neighbouring engine and the starboard undercarriage dangling from its bay. He was also able to see a large M on the side of the fuselage.

"Sparks?"

"Yes, skipper."

"Use the aldis and send signal to M-Mother and ask if there is anything we can do. And tell him the starboard undercarriage is dangling from its bay."

A short while later an aldis started blinking from the astro dome of the other aircraft. Sparks spoke the message as he read it. "M-Mother says she has lost the starboard outer engine. Thinks constant speed unit is u/s. Can't feather propeller. Am about to close down inner engine because of a fire warning light. Have also tried to get dangling undercart back up on the hand pump, but without success. Engineer thinks the reservoir has been holed. Offer to help much appreciated. But you can no do. Suggest you press on, D-Dog. We'll be okay."

HC said, " Send reply: We'll escort you till we are out of range of night fighters. Then say Per Ardua Ad Astra in farewell."

They accompanied the stricken Halifax over half way across the North Sea. Wished them luck and went on ahead and landed at Beeston.

The fate of M-Mother was just one of the many tragedies to emanate from the war. The captain and the engineer, on approaching Beeston, concluded that there were too many hazards confronting the Halifax in carrying out a piloted landing, the dangling undercarriage, and only half the power and, now, they discovered they had a wing flap floating in the wind. The skipper ordered the crew to take to their parachutes and before the engineer baled out he got him to open the escape hatch in the roof of the cockpit. An icy, roaring gale of air, past the hatchway almost drowned the noise of the surviving engines. The engineer made his escape through the floor hatch in the nose section of the fuselage.

The captain, satisfied the rest of the crew was parachuting to earth, decided that it was his turn to abandon the aircraft. In its crippled state he got it heading out across what he thought to be open country. It took him some time to trim the Halifax and engage the autopilot. And even then it wandered about unpredictably. He wondered if it would fly level long enough for him to get out of his seat and out through the top hatch. He eased himself slowly out of his seat. The Halifax yawed to the right; he was tempted to get back in the seat. Instead he hurried to the hatch and clipped on his parachute. He hauled himself up through the hatch and was lashed by the rushing wind. As he did so the Halifax lurched to the right. The force leaned him over the side of the fuselage and he had a precarious sensation of looking down into a dark void. He thought he saw the tail unit slipping around to his right and the tip of a wing disappearing in a black hole. Fearing that the Halifax was about to roll over and spin to earth he crawled away from the hatch, went over the side of the fuselage, down onto the shoulder of the wing and slipped into space over the trailing edge. And parachuted to safety.

A fortnight later the poor fellow, wracked by guilt and remorse, took his own life after it was reported what really happened that night. It transpired that had he landed the Halifax in its crippled condition and forfeited his life in the process he would have been the only casualty. Whereas by leaving the Halifax to its own devices, it had spun in on a small hamlet destroying three cottages and killing some nine inhabitants in their beds.

The tragedy had a huge impact on HC. Out of loyalty and compassion to a fellow officer, which he claimed Harvey Fenton had nurtured in him he lead a delegation of officers to Mellows, their squadron commander, and requested that the death of the officer be reported as killed on operations. The highest authority in Bomber Command sanctioned it. And the messes at Beeston chipped in for the headstone. It read:

Wings Upon the Night

Royal Air Force
Beeston

Here lies a warrior of the night
Who lost his life on operations
in the service of his country on
10th March 1943
Flt. Lt. Richard Sheldon
Skipper of M-Mother

Seven

Wing Commander Herby stood looking out of a window of his office. The landscape of fields and country lanes, and trees and hedgerows fell away in a twenty-degree slope to Beeston some three miles distant. Very often he could see the aircraft by day lifting off above the hedges and trees and returning later from an air test to slope back over the hedges and trees to land. The crew had been up to check the aircraft and equipment in readiness for a forthcoming operation. At night he often watched them setting out on a raid. And returning several hours later, still in darkness. But he could only see them as moving lights, red, green and white in colour. Sergeant Cinders came in behind him and said, "Flying Officer Hadley-Chase has arrived, sir."

Herby turned to her, "Thank you, Sergeant. Show him in, if you will."

HC came in and saluted in spite of the fact Herby was not wearing his cap. Cinders went out and closed the door.

"Right young man, grab a pew and smoke if you wish."

HC said: "I tried a pipe once and ended up turning green and getting large ulcers on my tongue."

"Cigarettes?" Herby laughed.

"I went dizzy each time I tried those."

"Well, to start with, I must congratulate you on the success of the operation the other night when I came with you. And your crew – what a splendid team."

"Thank you, sir."

Herby leant forward in his chair, "Also, you are to be commended for the manner in which you dealt with the demise of flight lieutenant Sheldon. It was a very gallant gesture on your part including your choice of headstone."

HC said, "I hear that some, further up the chain of command, were not impressed. At group level in particular."

"I think that was because the civilian authorities wanted to make something out of the matter. Take revenge, as it were, on the air force that, they claimed, had killed those eighteen civilians. But big daddy of Bomber Command stepped in and authorised your request which, he described as exemplary. He added that the civilian authorities would do well to consider how they might have reacted had the doomed bomber been a Heineken or a Downier." Herby paused to put a match to his pipe. Got it going and blew a cloud of smoke into the air. "Now we come to the main reason why I asked to see you.

When you were posted to Beeston, do you know how you ended up with sergeant Bosanquet as a second pilot in your crew when all other crews only had a single pilot?"

"Well, sir, as I remember, Sergeant Bosanquet actually nominated me as the captain and, in fact, he rounded up all the others including the navigator. I was greener than grass and really didn't have a clue what was going on. But I can tell you this: I was more than grateful to have Bosey along. I will go so far and say that had it not been for him the whole crew might have perished during one of my hazardous night landings."

Herby nodded, "I know. You wrote of your concerns to your mother, did you not?"

HC sat erect in his chair, "Yes, I did. And I discovered during my last leave that she wrote to the air force about it. I was not best pleased."

Herby said, "I can assure you that she was very discreet. And there were only three of us in the service who knew about it. Me, your squadron commander, Mellows, and Bosey."

HC frowned as something crossed his mind. "Did you say my mother wrote to you?"

"Yes. She did."

"Then you must be my father. She mentioned something about having a fling, as she called it, with an officer of the Royal Flying Corps and during which I was conceived. She said you went to Canada and then came back just before the war started. And that you were currently serving as a wing commander."

Herby said, "Now, I suppose, you'll probably want to ask me all the proverbial questions. Like, why I didn't marry your mother? Why did I desert her? And did I not consider the stigma of a bastard being attached to you owing to the fact you were born out of wedlock?"

HC said: "I'm too mature to worry about things like that. I've had a good life. Mother, and Horace, made sure of that. Do you know? Mother has never condemned you. She said it takes two to tango, whatever you make of that?"

"Then you are not offended?"

"Not at all. A little shocked, perhaps. But not annoyed. Is there anything else I should know?"

Herby said very cautiously, "Well, there is. Though it is not connected with your mother." He hesitated. Was it fair to give the boy another shock in such a short space of time, he asked himself.

HC smiled, "I'm waiting."

"The fact is, Peter, I've been looking through the records, in recent days, of Sergeant Bosanquet. Bosey as you call him. And it would appear he is your step brother."

"How come?"

"I was serving in the Royal Flying Corps, in the last war, when I had a relationship with a young French girl by the name of Michelle Bosanquet. She had a child by me."

"Out of wedlock, was it?"

"Yes. I'm afraid it was."

"Goodness gracious, father! You must have been the scourge of the Flying Corps where any young maiden was concerned. How can you be sure about Bosey?"

"His name, his date of birth and the fact he is so much like your paternal grandfather, Samuel Herby. Medium height, firmly built, dark hair and eyes and moustache. And, of course, his liking to get on the wing."

"I tried a moustache once." HC grinned. "Mother made me remove it, saying it looked ridiculous. She said it looked like a scattering of bum fluff."

They laughed about it for some time. Then Herby said, "What made you join the air force?"

"Well, mother, said your family had flying in the blood. So there was a good chance I had it in the genes. I'd always been keen on all things flying. I'd sit and watch the gulls when they came in scavenging off the land or followed the plough. Also I enjoyed watching the rooks build their nests, each year, high up, in the elms or the poplars. And when the young were ready they'd pitch off the nest on their first solo. That was a treat in itself to watch. And then, of course, I got involved with falconry at a young age and hunted with two birds."

" How many hours dual did you do before you went solo?"

" Eight."

"That was good."

"Was it?"

"Yes. I don't think many do it under twelve hours."

"I wasn't so good when it came to night flying. It was more the case of hold on tight, close my eyes, and hope for the best."

They both laughed for a time about that.

"Well, I must say your landing the other night was spot on. There's not many, some with more hours than you, who can three-point a heavy. Did you find out what you were doing wrong in the early days?"

"Not really. I went home for a spot of leave. Met a pretty girl. And came back and everything fitted into place. If anything I think Jenny made me more relaxed and more confident."

"Have you proposed to her?"

"Yes. And she has accepted. I've applied for leave."

Herby looked at his watch and stood, "Congratulations! I shall be writing to your mother to tell her of our meeting today, if that's all right with you?

"That's fine. There is just one further point. When do you propose to tell Bosey that you are his father and I am his step-brother."

"He is seeing me later today. How do you think he might react? Be angry? Or possibly deny my claims?"

"Knowing Bosey he will probably be amused. Especially when he learns you were the scourge of the RFC and all those maidens you bedded, father."

Herby thrust his hand forward to grip his son's hand in farewell. "Thank you my boy for taking the news of your origins in good spirit."

HC donned his cap and with a huge grin on his face fetched up a snappy salute. And left the room.

Sergeant Cinders came in after he had departed. She closed the door and said, "How did he take the news?"

Herby turned to face her. He said, "He took it very well in the circumstances; no signs of bitterness that I could detect. He did accuse me, however, of being the scourge of the Royal Flying Corps and all the local maidens."

"And were you?" Cinders smiled.

"The truth is, Polly, I fathered two other children, out of wedlock, a boy and a girl. The boy is here at Beeston. It's flight sergeant Jaque Bosanquet. The chances of us all ending up here together, after all these years must have been in the order of a million to one. Jaque's mother was a French girl. And then there was Charlotte, a nurse. She had a daughter by me."

Sergeant Cinders was not totally surprised by his confessions. He had that ruggedly handsome look about him and had a charisma that drew women to him. It wasn't in what he said but more in the way he looked at you with warm, brown eyes and that engaging smile. She was only too aware that she was very fond of him and physically drawn to him. She had never seen him in the nude and probably never would. But it did not stop her from fantasising in the privacy of her living quarters where she imagined him to have a broad, deep chest, a slim torso and handsome loins, and a profile that resembled that of a buffalo. She blushed every time she got too close to him and regularly had to go to a bathroom to cool down.

She had led a rather sheltered life. Her early education was at a convent school. And on leaving school her parents paid for her to attend a secretarial college. She graduated with very good speeds in shorthand and typing. But unlike a lot of girls her age she had never enjoyed any social life, nor had a boyfriend. Her parents: father, a court clerk and mother, a housewife, never encouraged it. And, sometimes, she desperately yearned for a bit of romance in her life to satisfy the dictates of her thoughts and feelings, which gathered pace when she reached puberty.

Her first position in employment was that of a secretary to the managing director of a company that made biscuits of both the plain and sweet variety. She'd been there for a year when Britain declared war on Germany and conscription to the services began. Polly used it as an excuse to leave home, and her over-protective parents, to go out into the wider world. Like most young people of her age she yearned for her independence.

She joined the Air Force and was rather amused to discover that her basic training was conducted in much the same atmosphere as her days at the convent school – it was all women. When she moved on to her trade training, secretarial and administration, she got to know the air force terms and jargon. But in all other subjects she was miles ahead of the others on the course, including most of the instructors.

From training she was posted to Wing HQ at Beeston as Administration Assistant to Wing Commander T. Herby. Over the weeks she learnt from his adjutant that he was married, that he was quite a few years older than her and that he had lost a son, Paul, to the war.

"Are you all right, Polly?" he broke into her thoughts.

"Oh, yes. I'm sorry, sir. I was miles away."

"I was saying I've got a few letters to dictate."

"Yes, I'm ready." She sat by his desk, pencil and shorthand pad poised.

Three days later HC went off to marry Jenny the land girl. He wanted Bosey to be his best man. But for some obscure reason Bosey couldn't get leave. He ended up having Horace for the part.

A number of Halifax's were grounded at this time, D-Dog being amongst them. Urgent modifications were carried out in an attempt to cure the bombers of their excessive weight problem and improve their operational ceiling. Bits and pieces of superfluous internal structure and equipment were removed, as was the big heavy mid upper gun turret.

Maurice Clarke was thrown into panic when the ground crew told him what they were up to, under the supervision of Handley Page engineers. As he saw it the removal of the turret would make him superfluous to the requirements of the crew. It worried him so much he put off going off on leave with the others. But with them gone he could find no one who could tell him what was going on. Eventually and with great relief he found Bosey who had taken over the captaincy of the crew whose officer had committed suicide.

"What's the matter young Maurice?"

"A lot of things. They're taking the top turret out of D-Dog. The rest of the crew has gone on leave. And the skipper hasn't told me how I stand. It looks as if I'm being elbowed out."

Bosey said, "I think you'll find that Stan Sparks has volunteered to stand down and let you take on the job of wireless operator. You did a WOP course before you joined the crew didn't you?"

"Yes, I did. And it was you, Bosey, who got me chasing the armourers for more gen on the guns. And visiting the W/T section to get my deciphering up to speed."

"Have you still got the Morse key in your room?"

"Yes. But I haven't used it a lot recently."

Bosey put a fatherly hand on his shoulder. "I suggest you practice and get your sending and receiving back up to speed before the others get back from leave."

Maurice almost cried with relief. "Yes Bosey. I will, I will. I promise. Thanks a lot for letting me know the score." And he hurried back to his quarters, rigged up his Morse key and began practicing in earnest.

Bosey had declined the offer to be HC's best man and remained at Beeston for a good reason. He visited a local farmer to organise the rental of a cottage for the newlyweds as a surprise when they returned. He paid a couple of WAAFs to give the place a good clean and he stocked it with food for the couple's arrival.

The cottage was only three miles from the aerodrome boundary and two miles south of the centre line of the east/west runway. As a result it was subjected to the thunderous and roaring activities of the Beeston bomber force night and day. The couple ignored it, or, more possibly was deaf to it so engrossed were they in each other, bound by a deep affection that had become the dominant force in their young lives. Nothing else mattered. The world was their oyster. And in her role as wife and homemaker Jenny made a few small changes in the cottage. She added little cushions to the settee and armchairs. Laid a number of rugs. Made some gathered, full length curtains. Displayed a variety of ornaments on small lace mats and hung landscapes, painted in oils, on blank, distempered walls.

Their life became a succession of partings and greetings with the young, radiant Jenny always there to send him off on a raid with a few quiet words of reassurance. And to welcome him home with open arms and a smile that did much to purge him of the toil, sweat and strain that he incurred from the bombing operations. In his absences she had Groocho, a four-year-old black Labrador who they adopted after its owner failed to return from a raid on Essen.

The cottage also became a home-from-home for the aircrew and ground crew and their lady friends. And HC and Jenny regularly hosted parties there They played party games and danced in the garden under the stars whilst a gramophone played music and song through an open window. They generally let their hair down and lived life to the full and till it was over-brimming. And they ignored the progress of the war so as not to lose a precious moment of it.

Croker and Clarke got back to their quarters after flying their third operation with HC as the skipper and Maurice's third trip as wireless operator. Getting married to that Jenny girl had changed the skipper almost beyond recognition. His dodgy night landings were definitely a thing of the past and he had brought his own brand of leadership to bear by introducing his own little patter when addressing the crew in flight. He called them: rear-gun, sparks, engines, and bombs. He made one exception and that was possibly because Fenton was a fellow commissioned officer. Sometimes he called him navigator but mostly he called him Harvey.

In the room they shared the two gunners stripped off their trousers and battle tops and shirts and vests and took their turn at the wash basin to rinse their faces. Croker also brushed his teeth. Clarke got into bed and lay hands behind his head looking up at the ceiling. He waited for Davey to get in the adjacent bed where he sat leaning against the head frame, smoking a cigarette.

"Davey, what do you know about the orderly in the sick bay?" He was both intrigued and had become obsessed with the effeminate nursing orderly who had treated him recently.

"Which one? There's three of them."

"The one who looks, talks and moves like a woman."

Croker turned and grinned. "That's Gloria!"

Clarke raised himself suddenly and rested on an elbow, "Gloria! He's a bloke isn't he?"

Croker drew heavily on the cigarette and exhaled a long stream of smoke. "From what I've heard, Gloria is something of a freak of nature. It's quite tragic, really."

"What do you mean, a freak of nature?"

"Well – the story goes that he was born as a girl. But some six months into his life he sprouted a Willy. However it did not develop as the rest of him developed. He's lucky if he can muster three inches, and an inch girth at full stretch. And that gets hidden by his pubic hair." He paused again to inhale from his cigarette. "His chest also has twin lumps shaped like a woman's breast and he has very big nipples. Much bigger than mine."

"How d'you know all this?"

"I was in the showers when he came in some months back. The poor bloke felt very conscious when he saw how the rest of us were equipped."

Clarke said," Hasn't he got big lips? Like those big, buxom blondes on the pin-up posters."

" He does use a smear of lipstick, you know, if you look closely."

"Yes I did notice. And I also noticed the skin on his face is very smooth and fine as if he doesn't need to shave."

Croker raised an eyebrow, "Did you take a fancy to him?"

Maurice felt the colour rise to his face and said, "Of course not! But he did leave me a bit confused. You know, whether he is a woman or a man?"

Croker said, "What I've seen, and heard, I think he's got the hormones of a woman. And that's why he behaves as he does." He stubbed his cigarette out in an ashtray on his bedside locker; "The story goes that his family kicked him out because he was a freak. An aunt took him in and steered him into hospital work when he left school. He joined the air force when the war started. And even the senior medical officers, here, admit he is good at his job."

"What really is his job, Davey?"

"He specialises in VD, venereal disease, that attacks all our bits and pieces in the crutch, a thoroughly nasty business. We ordinary rankers get it off the women, they say. And the officers get it from sitting on dirty lavatory seats. Gloria is an expert on the disease." He paused. "Hey, don't you remember the films and lectures we got when we were square-bashing?"

Clarke said: "Gloria treated me a few weeks back."

Croker nearly choked in surprise at his revelation. "He treated you, Maurice! For what?"

"He said, I'd caught a dose."

Croker's laughter echoed loudly in the room and in the stillness of the night.

"Where, in hell, did you get it from?" he roared.

"I think I picked it up from a Tart on my last leave."

"Maurice, you amaze me. You'd be the last in the crew I'd expect to get caught."

"Well, I did. And Gloria has sorted me out, you'll be pleased to know."

Croker moved from the bed, "Ready for lights out?"

"Ready."

In the darkness, Croker said, " Gloria not only sorts out all the VD problems. They also use her to head up the recovery team that picks up all the bits and pieces when a kite comes back with dead and injured on board. She recovers the bodies and lays them out and helps the pioneer boys clean and disinfect the aircraft. A bloody gruesome job, they say and which our Gloria, does with great dignity and respect…"

"That's enough! I've heard enough gory details for tonight." Clarke ordered. "Goodnight Davey." He pulled the covers swiftly over his head to prevent himself from hearing more.

Maurice rapped the doorknocker of the dark shaped, slate roofed cottage. The door opened to Gloria, dressed as a woman. In consideration of the blackout regulations she drew him in and led the way along a dimly lit hallway, moving with narrow steps, swaying her hips and showing her shapely legs. They arrived in a small sitting room softly illuminated by a pastel green shaded table lamp. She stood with her back towards a mirror hanging over a small hearth in, which flames lapped leisurely around three small logs.

"Do you approve, Maurice?" she said in that soft, velvety voice of hers.

He stood admiring the transformation. It was obviously a wig she was wearing. But it was a good one. It covered her head with a bush of black tight curls that ended at her neck. She wore earrings, gold triangles, inset with a pearl that dangled on the end of a two-inch gold chain. She wore a delicate pink lipstick. Her midnight blue dress, printed with small yellow flowers, complimented her figure – the contours of her bust – her slim waist – and the delightful curve of her hips. He drew breath when he looked down and noticed her black stockings, possibly air force issue to the WAAF, which, gave prominence to her shapely legs and the delicate sweep of her ankles shaped, as the latter were, by her leather, black high-heel shoes.

"What can I say?" he said. " Only that you look stunning."

She moved to him and played with his hands. "Do you really mean it?" You don't think I look bit of a fraud?"

"Not a bit. It suits you."

She led him to a settee and sat him beside him, holding his hands.

" I invited you here, Maurice, because, one, we're on neutral territory and away from the prying eyes at Beeston. Two, I'm very fond of you. And, three, are you interested in having a meaningful relationship with me?"

Maurice's eyes travelled again from her black, shoes and up her black stocking covered, curvy legs to the hem of the dress that had risen three or four inches above her knees when she crossed her legs. He looked at the thin belt around her narrow waist and a little higher up her clothed breasts, her long neck in the V shaped collar of her dress and then that delicate smooth skin of her face.

"Yes, I am, Gloria." He gripped her hands.

"She squeezed his hand in appreciation of his agreement. "We shall have to lead a double life and be discreet and vigilant, you realise that? You'll have to be extra careful when we meet at Beeston and forget the name Gloria. My real name is Clarence Stanton."

"Sergeant – Clarence Stanton!" Maurice reminded her.

The name of Clarence didn't suit her at all in his opinion. And sounded even more unsuitable when she posed for him, later, in her lace-trimmed briefs and bra, suspenders belt and those delightful black stockings. She looked every bit the woman. Gloria suited her so much better. And when the lights went off she accommodated him with, perhaps, considerably more ardour, and finesse, and sincerity of purpose than Marlene, the street girl, had.

Over the ensuing months Maurice escorted her to all the parties held by the skipper and his wife at the cottage and nobody twigged her disguise. He thought Davey Croker might rumble her, especially the name of Gloria. But he never gave any signs of doing so. Probably it was because he was so wrapped up with Fiona. Gloria's superb wig and stylish dresses, her cracking legs and full, red lips drew a lot of attention. So much so, at times, that Maurice grew quite jealous when other males got too close to her.

The young woman in nurses uniform approached Marie Herby in the kitchen of Hadley Manor late one evening. "Mrs Herby?"

Marie turned and smiled, "Yes. That's me."

The nurse looked around to ensure they were alone and said, "May I introduce myself, I'm Helen Hogarth. And I would like to ask a favour of you. You are the wife of wing commander Timothy Herby, aren't you?"

"Yes. I am."

"Could you arrange for me to meet your husband in private?"

Marie looked at the shape of the face and the eyes nose and mouth; they were very familiar. Though she had no idea why they should be so.

She said, "It's not quite possible at the moment. He's working away for the air force, you see. I think he is due for some leave in a fortnight's time. But it's only for three or four days."

"Oh, that would be splendid if I could meet him then."

Marie, puzzled again by the familiarity of her face, said, "You said you wanted to speak to my husband in private. Is that right?"

"Yes, please."

"As his wife am I permitted to know why you must see him in private?"

The young woman blushed, " Not really. Well – that is not until after I've spoken to him." She paused and gave Marie a sympathetic smile. "I'm sorry if I appear devious and somewhat rude. But I assure you there are very good reasons."

"You haven't been here very long, have you?"

"Two weeks today."

Marie said, "Very well then I'll leave a message for you in the nurses quarters as soon as he arrives."

"Thank you so much, Mrs Herby. I'm very much obliged." the nurse said and left.

Marie stood and watched her leave, puzzled about the face, and suffering pangs of anguish; she had a deep-rooted suspicion that the young woman had a connection with her husband, Timothy's past.

Eight

The auditorium was filling up. A sign in block capitals above the closed curtains of the stage read: IN MEMORIAM. Down in the orchestra pit the musicians warmed and tuned their instruments: the squeal of a violin, some short blasts from a trumpet, the groan of a saxophone, the deep notes of a bass, a flurry of drum beats, the haunting strains of a clarinet, the groan of a trombone. Behind the footlights figures came and claimed their seats, ladies in gowns and men in evening dress or military uniform. There was a sprinkling of the army, a few naval officers, and the Royal Air Force who were in the majority. Here and there a lighter flame or a struck match flickered in the dim lighting and cigarette and cigar smoke drifted or lingered overhead.

The babble of voices fell quiet as the last of the audience took their seats and the lights dimmed. A fanfare of trumpets heralded the opening of the curtains, which disclosed the presence of an ebony bright grand piano and its stool standing centre stage. From the wings the MC emerged and stood before a microphone, elegantly dressed in white tie and black tailcoat.

"Ladies and gentleman welcome to IN MEMORIAM which, as it would suggest, is a concert in memory of a young flying officer, Paul Herby, who lost his life on flying operations about a year ago.

From the day he was born his mother tried to encourage him into music and at 7 years of age put him to the piano. But he rebelled after a short number of lessons. This was when the family lived in Canada. When war threatened his father brought the family to Britain and Paul followed in his father's footsteps and joined the Royal Air Force. He distinguished himself as a fighter pilot in the 1940 German Offensive by destroying twelve enemy aircraft and probably three others.

Following the end of the offensive he continued flying Spitfires but as an unarmed photographic reconnaissance pilot. And his mother says this is when he took to the piano and music inspired, she feels sure, by a young lady named Melanie. His mother is confident that it was also Melanie who brought the composer out in him.

Over a period of six months he wrote some twenty compositions and familiarised himself with the classics found in Debussy, Mozart, Chopin,

Rachmaninov and Tchaikovsky to name but a few. His mother rather hoped he would become a concert pianist at the end of the war and tour the world capitals." The MC wrung his hands, "But as we all know this was not to be. It was during her early months of grief, and her lament in private about this lost opportunity for him to make his mark on the world, that his mother was inspired by the work, he left behind, to do concerts in his memory. Marie Herby is not well known in the music world as a classical pianist. But I can assure you that once you have listened to this concert you will be enchanted and be in no doubt that she is a skilled and supreme musician. Her music will make you laugh and cry. It will sober you, humble you. Above all it will inspire you.

She would like to devote this concert, not only to her son, Paul, but also to all those mothers who have lost children to this war. The concert comes in three parts. The first deals with the composers mentioned earlier. The second part deals with Paul's own compositions with titles such as, Melanie, Come Gather Clover, and Cottage on the Hill, The Hadley Theme and The Twilight Concerto. And the third and final part covers the works composed by this talented and gifted lady herself." He turned and beckoned to the wings. "Ladies and gentlemen – I give you Mrs Marie Herby."

Marie walked elegantly on stage dressed in a pastel green gown reaching to the ankles, gold evening shoes, her fair hair rolled and pinned on the back of the head, eyes bright and smiling, her lips a delicate pink in colour."

Whilst the audience applauded, Marie curtsied and took her seat on the stool. As the clapping subsided she launched in to Tchaikovsky's: Piano concerto No. 1.

She followed it with Rachmaninov's: Rhapsody on a theme of Paganini.

Next came Grieg's: Piano concerto.

She played some pieces by Mozart and Beethoven.

And ended the first part of the concert with Claire De Lune by Debussy.

For this part alone she received a standing ovation. She stood before the audience fighting back the tears and trying to swallow a lump in her throat. When she looked up at a box to her right she saw a solitary young man in air force uniform, standing and clapping his hands boisterously, and smiling down at her. God! She thought. Is that Paul? But when she looked up again the box was empty. The MC called her off stage to take a break and the curtain fell.

She moved out of a side door of the stage and took another look up at the box. To discover it was empty. "What's the matter?" the stage manager asked her.

"I thought I saw somebody up in the box. A young air force officer. And I do know he wasn't there when the show started."

"Nobody booked any of the boxes tonight, Marie."

She went to the ladies to freshen up. Drank a cup of tea and waited in the wings for the MC to announce the second part of the concert. She walked on stage to another warm and rousing reception from the audience. She looked up at the box. It was empty and in darkness as were all the other boxes.

She launched into Paul's composition, " Melanie".

Melanie sat in the front row of seats, flanked by Marie's wing commander husband and flying officer Hadley-Chase to her left and flight sergeant Bosanquet to her right. The three men had arrived that afternoon from Beeston and been greeted by Lady Hadley who knew Peter, Mollie Langdon's son, sired by Timothy Herby. But she had never met Jaque Bosanquet. And as soon as she saw him she marvelled at his likeness to the Herby family especially his grandfather Samuel in Canada. Medium height, robust chest and torso, strong, capable hands and he had a presence that was almost spiritual. You could be in a room and have your back to him. But you knew he was there. His dark features and moustache made him very approachable and very desirable by women, Claire Hadley thought. Though it was very doubtful if he ever considered himself anything of the sort. Like previous generations of the Herby family he came over as a modest and a dependable sort of person.

Marie Herby's first meeting with the two young men had been a little strained at first principally because they were not her children. They were her husband's boys from relationships he'd had with other women during the First World War. They were also painful reminders of her son, Paul, who she had lost to the present war. They might compensate for the loss of Paul where her husband was concerned. But for her they did not. They only served to sharpen Paul's loss.

Lady Hadley had told her in private, that afternoon, that it was quite improper of her to condemn the two boys. They had not asked to come into the world. And the two mothers she despised so much were not to blame either. The two boys had been conceived before she married Paul. She should, out of respect to her late parents, and the sisterhood of women, accept the boys into the family circle.

Marie acted on the advice and made herself cordial and well mannered to the two young men. But she did not find it easy.

After the concert, following a long ovation, and time for her to sign autographs they had supper in the Thespian Court, a popular eating house in Oxford. They drove back to Hadley in the manor's shooting brake where they dropped Lady Hadley, Marie and Melanie off at the manor. Timothy Herby drove his two sons up to the cottage on the hill, their accommodation for the night and where they'd dropped their bags earlier in the day. He prodded the fire into life and added more logs. He amused his sons when he groped around to light the oil lamps. The place was so far behind the times, log fires, oil lamps, water from a garden well and rocking chairs. Bosey put a kettle of water on the fire and his father told him where everything was to brew some tea. Timothy brought a large journal from the sleeping quarters and put it on the sitting room table. Then they all loosened their shoelaces, took off their air force tunics, slackened their neckties and took to the chairs in the homely light of the lamps and flickering firelight.

With mugs of tea to hand Timothy spent the next hour enlightening them with the history of the Herby family dating back to the pioneering flights of Willy Herby and then coming up through the next two generations of him and his father who likewise took to the wing and then Samantha, their great aunt. He brought the story right up to date by explaining their connection with the family tree and what it would mean to their paternal grandfather in Canada. He showed them pictures of the glider and powered kites painted in oils by Lady Hadley. He showed them hand-drawn sketches of Willy Herby in flight with his flimsy wing in the West Country. They read extracts from the journal that recorded the pioneering flights made by Timothy and his father.

They slept for only four hours that night before Timothy roused them and they washed and shaved. And he took them out and showed them around the hill and the paddock from which he and his father had made their experimental flights before they went down the manor for breakfast. The morning was spent touring what was left of the Hadley estate. He showed them his old school, the trout streams and the Hadley farmland. He led them through the Hadley woods and they were taken aback to come across a mound of earth, overgrown with grass, marked with a solitary crude wooden cross.

"Is this the grave of a mortal?" Peter said. "If so it's a bit bizarre."

Timothy said, ""I didn't know this existed till after we moved to Canada. My father told me about it and, having done so, said he never wanted to talk about it again. He felt in some way responsible for this man's death. His name was Jake Howson a poacher of these parts. But he did not get killed for his illegal activities. Evidently it was a slip of the tongue. My father, your grandfather, was socialising with the squire's wife of an evening as part of an agreement made between the three people involved. They spent the evening with a band of travelling folk. And on their way back to the manor at dawn they chanced to stop on the banks of the trout streams and indulge in a little coitus. The poacher, on his way home from a successful foray into the estate's land of abundant game, spotted and identified the couple and told his friends in his local village inn. Before long the gossips spread the word and it becomes common knowledge.

The Squire and Lady Hadley were so humiliated, and frantic about their reputation, the Squired hired hands to have the poacher put down and interred, out of sight, in the woods. Evidently your grandfather and my wife's father were delegated to carrying out the clandestine burial."

"What made grandfather Herby feel so guilty about it?" Peter asked.

"From what he said, he should not have been out on public view with Lady Hadley that night and early morning. They should have stayed in the manor. And had they done so the poacher would not have made the observation and laid claim to their amorous and improper behaviour."

"But did you say there was some sort of agreement between the Squire, his wife and grandfather? If so, what was it?"

"The Squire and Lady Hadley had tried, unsuccessfully, for years to start a family. So I think, in desperation, he approached grandfather Herby and proposed he do the honour for him."

"And did grandfather succeed?" Peter interrupted.

"Yes. He and Lady Hadley conceived Samantha."

Peter looked across at Jaque and winked, "I would have thought the Herby men would have done better by starting a stud farm instead of trying their arm at flying. What says you brother?" He led the way out of the woods, smiling, and they made their way back toward the manor. On the way they went into the cemetery and were shown the grave of their great aunt, Samantha. And the headstone erected in memory of their stepbrother Paul. Both the young men found it a humbling experience in the cool, spiritual silence of the church yard in which the only sound came from a robin perched on a Holly bush. It sang to the world with all the trilling poise and perfection of a nightingale. And it was truly magical in that such a volume of song would come from such a small creature

They moved inside the church and they saw the brass plate referring to the memory of Lieutenant George Sawyer, Observer, R.F.C. Killed on active service in support of the Battle of Mons 5th June 1916. Herby explained that it was his wife's father.

Jaque Bosanquet said, "So there was flying blood in the Sawyers too?"

His father said, "I think in George's case it was more a case of patriotism and a spirit of adventure. Although it is true to say he did go aloft with your grandfather in the glider and powered kite we constructed. And he seemed quite at home up there. I also took his daughter, Marie, up with me a couple of times and I must say she was a good navigator. It was as instinctive to her as it is to a bird."

They filed into one of the pews and for several minutes sat in silence, gazing up at the stained-glass windows and the graceful curving arches in the roof. A scent of incense floated around on the still, cool air The peace and sanity of the atmosphere came as balm to the least hint of a troubled mind. It helped to draw away the haze of worry floating behind the eyes and in the thoughts: the quiet unsaid anxiety of the dangers of the war, the fear of a premature death, the dread of losing or being parted from a valued friend.

After lunch at the manor Peter and Bosey went off alone to talk to the military patients. Timothy Herby stood alone in the spacious study made comfortable by the presence of a large oak desk and two leather armchairs. Opposite the desk a log fire burned brightly and, at times, a little noisily in a large hearth. Lady Hadley had told him to use the room for the meeting that Marie had arranged for him. He stood looking out of the window, smoking a pipe, pondering.

A little before three he heard voices in the hall. They stopped on reaching the study entrance and there were tapping sounds on the study door. He bid the visitor to enter and the door opened to his wife and a young woman.

"Timothy, this is Miss Helen Hogarth who wishes to speak to you in private. Miss Hogarth may I introduce you to wing commander Herby."

The young woman waited for Mrs Herby to leave and close the door behind her before she faced her husband. He beckoned her toward him and shook her hand in greeting. Then showed her to one of the leather armchairs. He noticed she had a lot of her mother about her except, perhaps, for the chin, nose and brow, which were features of the Herby family. He said, "Before you say anything, I think I know the reason why you wanted to see me. Are you trying to trace your father?"

Helen smiled, self-consciously; she had not expected him to get to the point so quickly. "Well – yes – but," she stammered.

He said, "Is your mother's name, Charlotte?"

She nodded. To which he added, "And were you born in 1918?"

"Yes,"

He regarded her with admiration in his eyes and a fatherly smile on his lips. "You are so much like your mother. I noticed it the moment you entered the room. And I see by your uniform you have followed her into the nursing profession." He got out of his chair and came around the desk and reached for her hands, "It's an honour to have such an attractive daughter. And it might sound trite of me to apologise for neglecting you and your mother all these years." Helen felt a lump growing in her throat and her eyes threatened to pump tears. She pulled herself up and leant against him, hiding her face on his chest. He said, "I did invite your mother back to Hadley, with you. And where you would have been well looked after but…"

"I know – I know," she interrupted, almost in a whisper. "Mother told me all about it. And how you got her reconciled with her parents."

"How is your mother, Helen?"

"Very well. My grandparents are no longer with us. My mother inherited the house when they passed on."

"Is she still nursing?"

"Yes. She is a theatre sister with one of those units that is pioneering burns surgery. She's very involved and very busy."

"Did she ever marry?"

"No. I've suggested it to her on many occasions. But she says she is quite happy. She enjoys her work and is satisfied that she gave me a good start in life."

Timothy eased her slightly away from him and handed her a handkerchief to wipe her damp eyes and blow her nose.

"Yes," he said. "She has made a good job of that, I can see."

She put the handkerchief in a pocket, saying she would return it to him, laundered. "Do you know," she added. "Mother keeps a photograph of you and her on her bedside table. I think it was taken when she nursed you in hospital. In France wasn't it?"

"Yes. It was. A hospital near Lyon."

She moved closer to him again. "Is that where I was conceived? In France I mean?"

"Hasn't your mother told you?"

" I didn't think to ask her. She told me, of course, that I was born in England."

He was spared from answering the question by tapping sounds on the study door and in walked a female member of the catering staff bearing a tray of tea, saying she had been instructed to bring it by Mrs Herby. She went through the motions of pouring and serving the tea, replenished the teapot with hot water, replaced the tea cosy and left. Timothy turned both armchairs towards the fire and sat alongside his daughter. "I think you should know, Helen, and I hope you won't be offended, that you have three step brothers. One of whom was killed on flying operations, about a year ago."

Her eyes lit up. "I have three brothers! That's incredible. I always wanted a sister or a brother."

"You did notice I said STEP brother?"

"But, of course. Mother never had any more children, she told me." She grew quite excited. "Who are they? Where are they? And what are their names?"

"Paul was the one who got killed. The other two are Peter and Jaque. They are pilots in Bomber Command."

"Do they know of my existence?"

"Only vaguely. And, by the way, you have grandparents who live in Canada."

"Do they know about me?"

"Not as yet. But now that I've located you I intend to write and tell them about you and your two step brothers." He paused and said, "Are you free this evening?"

"Yes. I'm not on duty again till tomorrow night."

"How would you like to join us for dinner this evening? You'll be a guest of Lady Hadley and her close friends."

"Oh, I don't know. I don't have a dinner dress. They are all at home."

"I'm sure you have a suitable dress. It'll be an informal occasion. Your brothers will be in uniform."

Helen wrung her hands. "I'm so excited. What time shall I arrive?"

"We'll gather in here for drinks at seven thirty. And for you to meet your brothers."

Helen stood on tiptoe and reached up and kissed him lightly on the face. "Thank you," she said.

"Thank you for what?" He grinned down at her.

"For being my father: a handsome and kindly man." She turned to go, hesitated, and turned back. "I told your wife that I would explain everything after I had the meeting with you. But on reflection I think it would be better coming from you. Don't you?"

"Yes, of course, Helen."

She went back her quarters and selected a dress and shoes for the evening. And sat down and wrote to her mother in rather excited scribble about the meeting with her father and the imminent meeting with her stepbrothers Peter and Jaque.

She arrived at the study at the appointed time and walked into a room bubbling with conversation. In the hearth flames from the burning logs reached up inside the chimney breast, she noticed. And a hand of each of the guests was holding a goblet Her father came and greeted her and took her to be introduced to Lady Hadley, an elderly, gracious lady who greeted her warmly and told her she must use the Manor as her second home. "Any friend or relative of the Herby family is a friend of mine, my dear."

Her father moved her on to meet his wife who seemed much more at ease than the first time they met. "May I cordially and officially welcome you to the family, Helen. And may I introduce you to Melanie, Paul's widow."

Helen, touched by their warmth and sincerity, shook their hand, in turn, and thanked them.

Then she was introduced to an elegantly dressed lady and her husband. "Welcome to Hadley, Helen." Mollie Hadley-Chase took her hand in greeting and kissed her lightly on the face. And presented her to her husband.

Helen couldn't help blushing; she was quite overwhelmed by their generosity and politeness.

Her father took her by the arm and led her across the room to two uniformed figures standing by the hearth. "Helen, meet your brother Peter and Jaque. Gentlemen this is your sister Helen." The appropriate greetings and handshakes were made and Peter said, "You're the only one without a drink, Helen. Would you care for some Champers?"

"Just a little, thank you."

In his absence to fetch it for her Jaque said, "What does your mother think about the circumstances of your origins? My mother never forgave him."

"Oh my mother, she was, and still is, very philosophical about it. She claims she came to consider me as a 'love child'. She said it happened at the peak of her desire, as a woman, to have a child…"

"Here you are, Helen, a little bit of fizz," Peter interrupted and handed her the glass of Champagne.

Their father proposed a Toast to lady Hadley for arranging the dinner. And then they all drank to Peter Jaque and Helen as new members to the Herby family. The dinner gong sounded and they went through to the dining hall.

Lady Hadley and Melanie stood looking discreetly through a window at Marie, Mollie and Helen making their farewells to Timothy and the boys as they prepared to return to Beeston by car.

"What a pleasant family!" Melanie remarked. "What a pity Paul died before he met his brothers and sister."

Lady Hadley said, "Had it not been for the war I don't think they would have found their father. Timothy said himself that it was a million to one chance of those boys arriving on the same R.A.F Station as him. And the same applies to you, Melanie."

"How do you mean, Lady Hadley?"

"Timothy only came to back to do his bit for Britain in the war. Paul joined him as you know and he ends up on an aerodrome near your roadhouse where you two met and started your liaison. And all that happened thereafter in your life was because of the war." They paused in the conversation to look through the net curtains at Marie embracing and kissing Timothy in farewell. Then she moved on to each of the boys with Mollie and Helen following on behind her.

The boys gave Helen a big hug. Her face went very red, her eyes glistened and her teeth sparkled white in quiet delight.

"Don't they get on well?" Melanie observed.

Lady Hadley nodded and they watched as the engine started and the car moved off along the driveway, arms waving from three of the windows. Marie, Mollie and Helen waved energetically back until it turned out of the main entrance and disappeared amongst the surrounding countryside.

On their return to the manor Melanie took round a tray of sherry.

"When do you think we'll see them again, Timothy." Lady Hadley inquired.

Timothy said, " At dinner last night they suggested that we all meet up again at the manor at Christmas. That is if the Lady of the Manor approves."

"It's perfectly acceptable to me. I'd consider it an honour. But Marie and Mollie might have other plans for the festive season." She motioned toward the two women.

Mollie said, "We'd be able to get away for a couple of days. But I wonder if Jenny would be able to cope with the travelling. She'll be seven months pregnant by then. For certain Peter would not leave her on her own over Christmas."

Lady Hadley said, " And you Marie? Have you made any arrangements?"

Marie said, " I would prefer to play it by ear. Peter and Jaque don't finish their tour of operations until some time in November. A lot can happen between now and then."

"I'm sorry Marie," Lady Hadley frowned. " I don't quite understand."

"What I mean, Claire, is that they are involved in very hazardous flying in Bomber Command. And I am reminded that we lost Paul not long before Christmas."

Lady Hadley came to her and put an arm around her. "Yes, I do understand. I'm sorry, Marie."

Mollie said, "If you'll excuse us, we'll be making out way back to the farm." She embraced the elderly, gracious lady and kissed her silver, grey hair. And Horace did likewise. They went to their laurel green Lagonda and waved a final farewell as it carried them along the drive.

Marie said, "Well, I must get back to my duties."

Helen said, "I'll go with you on my way back to my quarters." She was aware that Lady Hadley was about to take her afternoon nap; she had collected her wrap and picked up her cane and Melanie would escort her to her room.

The old lady said, "Please remember my dear you are most welcome to my home at any time you choose to visit."

Helen thanked her and gripped her frail hand gently in farewell And departed with Marie.

Lady Hadley turned to Melanie before they left the room, "Will you remind me tomorrow morning to write to Rebecca Herby in Canada."

NINE

Samuel Herby removed his flying jacket and flying suit, kicked off his heavy flying boots and trod into a pair of muclots, deerskin boots, that had been presented to him on one of the Indian reservations. He stored his flying togs neatly in a nearby locker and sat down at his desk and lighted his pipe. Phoebe, a half-breed, product of a Creote Indian mother and French father, worked as the office girl. Her long hair and distinctive black eyebrows and long eyelashes made her uniquely beautiful. She had excellent deportment and her smooth, gentle tongue served as a great tonic to the aging flying instructor. He knew she liked and respected him as a father figure, whereas he was aroused regularly by her presence. She brought to life in him a drive and passion that he thought had been taken from him in the process of getting old, and was not capable of being resurrected. Her mere presence made him rise to the occasion and which he discreetly hid from her. She came into his office with a pile of letters and a mug of tea laced with a measure of cognac, the latter of which was a privilege extended to all instructors, during the winter months, and when flying had finished for the day.

The Moths they were using for training were fitted with hoods as protection from the cold Canadian winter but the only cockpit heating they had was their heavy fleece-lined clothing. But as far as his job was concerned he reckoned he had the best at the Elementary Flying Training School.

His job was to take on pupils who had been ditched by their instructors for a variety of reasons. Lack of intelligence, incompetence, aptitude or merely poor co-ordination of mind and limb was often cited as the main reasons for being rejected.

The truth of the matter was that the instructors were under pressure to produce something that resembled a potential pilot within twelve hours of dual instruction.

He and Bill Cornell had realised early in their days of instructing that pupils came in about three different categories. The first group was naturally suited to flying and had a lively intellect to cope with the ground studies. The second group was not so well equipped, mentally, but they were passionate about flying and were hungry for knowledge. They heeded everything they were taught in the air and on the ground and never questioned anything. They became automated in their planning and in their actions, regimented and programmed, which fell in line with the wishes of their military superiors who dictated policy and the boundaries of discipline. They did however have a drawback in their regimentation. They lacked initiative in that if they got into a situation which they'd never come across before, either during flight or during their ground studies, they lacked the will and analytical expertise to deal with it.

The third group consisted of the cautious types. They did not readily accept everything they were taught particularly if theory was involved. They also found it difficult to absorb anything of an abstract nature. As an example the air being an invisible medium continually posed a challenge to their reasoning.

This caution manifested itself in making such characters seem slow and ponderous. But in his experience Samuel had found that many in the third group had been the victims of a personality clash between them and their instructors.

He had dealt with three such men that day and succeeded, using a mixture of humour, a fatherly touch and his renowned patience, in getting them off on their first solo after each of them had received an hour of his instruction.

Bill Cornell put his head in the office door and said, "Am I right in thinking you got them all through, Samuel. He was interested not only because of the reputation of the flying school but also because of the finances. The authorities only paid the school for pupils who completed the course. They never got a cent for the time they'd spent on a reject. That was why he and Samuel had come up with the idea of Samuel dealing exclusively with the rejects.

Samuel held his mug of tea up to him, "Every one a winner, Bill!" he declared.

Bill gave him a thumbs-up and said, "Thanks partner." And returned to his office.

Samuel wrote up his reports on the three pupils. Then tackled his mail, his fan mail as Phoebe smilingly called it. Which, in effect, it was when one considered it was mainly from pupils who had passed through his hands and were now at advanced flying schools. Or were now operational with the various commands under the umbrella of the Royal Air Force in England.

When he opened the letter from his son, Timothy, he couldn't quite understand what he was reading at first. He got to the bottom of the first page, shook his head, and returned to the start. The letter referred to a letter that he'd sent to Timothy just after Paul, his grandson, was killed, and he expressed his regret that the Herby family name was in danger of fading out.

In the letters that followed from Timothy, not once did he refer to his father's concerns. So Samuel decided that his son was either too embarrassed, or, plainly, not interested in the family's history.

And yet in this letter, before him, Timothy confessed to fathering three children, two boys and a girl, during the last war. He had not told him and mother before for fear of humiliating Marie. And he also thought if mother knew about it, it might open up some old wounds by reminding her of husband's affair with Lady Hadley and the conception of Samantha.

Samuel stopped reading for a moment and drew thoughtfully, and jubilantly, on his pipe. Three grandchildren indeed! That was quite something to ponder on and digest. Surely one of them would help to carry on the family name?

As he continued to read the letter his pride increased still more and he felt a measure of pride at learning that his two grandsons had followed the family tradition of taking to the wing. They were pilots serving with Bomber Command. His granddaughter had followed in her mother's footsteps and trained as a nurse. Timothy promised to send photographs of the children in his next letter.

He sank back in his chair and put another lighted match to his pipe just as Phoebe came in and asked if there was anything else she could do before she went home.

"No thanks, Phoebe. You can type up those student reports in the morning."

She came around the desk, stood by his chair and rested a hand on his shoulder. "Are you quite sure?"

He reached up and patted the hand on his shoulder, "Yes, thank you."

"Okay. See you in the morning, Samuel." She gave his shoulder an affectionate squeeze and glided out of the office, glancing over her shoulder and smiling warmly at him before she disappeared.

He was forced to put another match to his pipe. He read the letter through again and sat and pondered how he might break the news about the three other grandchildren to Rebecca.

Some months back she would have possibly been scathing about another scandal in the family. But, at the same time, Samuel felt it would be impossible for her to deny it was the seeds of her own son that had helped to conceive these offspring. They were part of her flesh and blood.

The only problem, now, was that Rebecca was no longer the woman she was. The death of Paul, their grandson killed in action just over a year ago had devastated her. She was morose, depressed and withdrawn, and had resigned as the ruler of the roost. He got home each day to find her lounging about in her nightdress. She didn't bother to put a brush or comb through her hair. She stopped washing regularly and, in fact, gave up on all her wifely duties. It had become so bad he was glad to get out of the house in the morning and reluctant to go home in the evening.

He sighed heavily, got up from the chair and dressed in a bearskin coat and beaver fur hat. He called out in farewell to Bill, his partner, in the adjacent office and set off for home trudging heavily and with a heavy heart.

Rebecca worked quietly in her small kitchen, concocting a moose casserole and a fruit trifle for Samuel's supper. Jazz music issued from a small speaker close to her and which had been relayed from the radiogram in the sitting room. For the very first time in what seemed an age, to her, she felt alive and was possessed of an urge to rally from the numbness and inactivity Paul's death had forced on her. It was a letter in her mail that morning that had provoked her into getting off her backside and pulling herself together. It wasn't so much from what the letter said but more so the shock of discovering whom it was from. Of all people it had to be Lady Claire Hadley who she always regarded as a rival.

Rebecca left the casserole on the oven top; she'd put it in to cook about an hour before Samuel was due home. She'd also put the trimmings on the trifle about that time. She luxuriated in a warm scented bath for nearly an hour and washed her hair. With a towel wrapped around her hair she went and stood naked before the full-length wardrobe mirror in her bedroom. She not only inspected herself for her own satisfaction; she needed to be assured that she still looked attractive to her husband who she had neglected badly over the last year whilst she had been locked in her grief for their beloved grandson, Paul.

Claire Hadley's missive reminded her sharply about Samuel's manly attributes and the child that he sired for her. It happened a long time ago but it still had occasion to rile her when something reminded her of it.

A look in the mirror disclosed areas of flabbiness and wrinkling that she had not seen before. Her breasts were sagging and her body hair had streaks of silver-grey like that on her head. "Don't be too hard on yourself," she spoke to the mirror. "You are, after all, approaching seventy five years of age."

She took from a drawer of her dressing table a liberty bodice she had got through Bill Cornell's wife, Angela. It was of French design, having come from a fashion house in Quebec. It was made of silk and consisted of quite large diamond shape netting and, unusually, had a tie from each of the breasts up to and around the neck. She put it on and the net pattern clung to her body and held it in shape and by altering the neck adjuster slightly it lifted the slightest hint of a sagging bust line. The bodice also allowed the body to breathe and the silk netting had rather a nice way of stimulating and massaging the skin.

She moved to the wardrobe and after sliding the gowns along the rail, inspecting them in turn, she decided on an old style, Royal blue in colour, that fashioned a most becoming bustle. She'd last worn it to a Ball before the war and had not forgotten the admiring glances and comments from the other male and female guests.

She hung the dress on the outside of the wardrobe and returned to sit at the dressing table where she shaped her hair in a Bouffant style that gave extra height and width to her hair by back-combing. Ladies at Royal Court had worn their hair like it for years and continued to do so as was shown in newspapers and fashion magazines.

By the time she finished the light was fading at the windows; it meant Samuel would be home in an hour. She took one more look at her hair and smiled agreeably at the silk net bodice. Her breasts had a distinct upward tilt and the netting design hid all her flab and wrinkles. She rolled on a pair of flame red stockings and held them in place with red white and black, laced trimmed garters.

The last time she paraded like this Samuel had ravaged her, she recalled with delight. Not only from the physical fulfillment she derived from it, and her role as the dutiful wife, but in her opinion she had also shown the memory of Claire Hadley that she too knew how to satisfy her man.

She trod into the dress, slipped her arms into the sleeves, buttoned the front, tied the waist and arranged the bustle at the rear and secured a blue cameo at the throat of her collar. She hurried downstairs and carefully put the casserole in the lighted oven, and put the trimmings on the trifle. She laid a table for two and dressed it with two lit candles and a carafe of wine. A small vase of flowers would have added a final touch of romance. But she had none. So, by way of compensation, she lit an oil lamp that was suspended over the table and switched off the electric light. The soft, orange glow from the lamp completed the scene. She felt very proud and anticipated the dinner preparations and the effort she had made to pull herself together would knock Samuel for six.

It did. He let himself in the front door looking grave and haggard until he discovered her waiting to greet him, smiling, and looking elegant and gracious in that Royal blue dress with its figure hugging lines that accentuated her breasts, her narrow waist and the French curves of her hips. He imagined her shapely legs, hidden by the dress, and wondered if she was wearing those flame red stockings and garters, and that silk net liberty bodice.

"How are you, my dear?" he held her gently and kissed her waiting lips.

"I'm fine, thank you, Samuel. How are you?"

"I'm a bit dumbfounded. Your hair – it's beautiful. And the dress! That's the one you wore to the annual Ball in British Columbia, is it not?"

Rebecca nodded.

"So what are we celebrating this evening?" he said.

Rebecca took him by the arm and led him to the foot of the stairs that led up to the bedrooms and bathroom. "Go up and wash and change. I'm taking you to dinner." She watched him, amused by the deep frown masking his face as he climbed the stairs; she was certain he had not fully grasped what was happening.

He had not; he came back down wearing his black tie and dinner suit on the basis that her dress, and invitation to dinner, warranted it. "What time is our carriage arriving?" he said. "Have we time for a drink before we go?"

Rebecca went to him. She held his hand and with her other free hand she held it against his face and looked sympathetically at him. "There's just the two of us, Samuel. And we are dining at home. Come now." She led him out of the hall, through the lounge into the soft orange light of the kitchen.

He sat and looked on in amazement as she draped a napkin across his lap and poured him a glass of medium sweet, white wine. She served the Mousse Casserole with dumplings to which he was more than partial. And the trifle had a generous taste of sherry.

Later they had cheese and biscuits and a fourth goblet of wine. He smiled at her. She smiled back at him. Beneath the table she kicked off her shoes and slid her feet up his trouser legs and rubbed against his ankles. Her face took on a distinct glow, replacing the strained, tired look of recent months. She continued smiling at him, relaxed and at ease with the world.

He said slowly, "Are you able to talk about Paul, now, without getting upset?"

She nodded, "I think the time has come to stop grieving for him, if that's what you think, Samuel. I won't forget him of course. I never shall. But, tell me, why do you ask?"

"Well, do you remember me always moaning about his passing and how it would bring the Herby family name to an end? Marie had come to the end of her childbearing days so there was no hope of Timothy and her producing another little Herby. And, you, I remember, were very upset because Paul was our one and only grandson.

I wrote to Timothy about it, your grief and my concern about the family name fading out because there were no more Herby males to carry it on. But he never acknowledged it in any of the letters he sent thereafter. Until today when I got a letter in the morning mail at the School."

Rebecca said, "All his past letters came to the house. Why not this time?"

"I'll let you read the letter. I think you'll find he didn't want to incur your wrath over what he's done." He took the letter and its envelope from inside his jacket and handed it to her. "Don't be too hasty and condemn him out of hand."

Rebecca withdrew the missive from its envelope, straightened the two folds and read. Timothy refilled their goblets with wine and studied her face, as she read. He made an attempt to interpret what was going through her mind.

She finished reading and she appeared to look through him, rather than at him. He reached across the table and put a hand on her hand. "What do you think, my dear?" he said quietly.

Rebecca said, "Do you think we'll ever see these other grandchildren?"

"I sincerely hope so. But I don't think it will be till after the war. Did you see in the letter where Timothy said he'd be sending us snaps of them in the next letter."

Rebecca looked vacantly across the table. "So both the boys are airmen. I'm very pleased for you Samuel. And the girl is a nurse. What did Timothy say her name is?"

"Helen."

" And Jaque Bosanquet? That's a French name, isn't it?"

"Yes. Timothy says in the letter the mother is French and the boy has her maiden name."

Rebecca said searchingly, "Who was this Mollie Langdon at Hadley? I don't remember her. The mother of Peter, so Timothy says."

"Oh that was the girl from the village, the one that the Hadleys cared for a lot. When her parents died they took her in and became her foster parents."

Rebecca pondered for a time then shook her head, "No, I'm sorry. I can't place her. Let's face it, it's forty years since we left Hadley." She got up from the table and went to him with an outstretched arm, "Come – let's dance." She led him to the lounge, pushed the furniture back to the walls and put a record on the radiogram. She switched off all the lighting, took and held his left hand, put his right hand behind her back, and placed her right hand on his shoulder. They danced slowly to the music of a string orchestra led by an unseen handsome, romantically inclined Mantovani whose recording discs Rebecca had collected since before the war. The music was both soothing and inspiring. They floated around the room with him leading, close, and intimate, in the flickering firelight.

They danced to six other discs of the music before they took a rest and sat before the hearth. Samuel lit a cigar and she brought glasses and an open bottle of the best Brandy. They had a measure each evening and had done so since they were in their late fifties. They considered it as a medicine that contributed to their ripe old ages.

She raised her glass to him, "To you, Samuel. For being so patient and caring since we lost Paul. I've neglected you badly and I apologise." She nudged her glass against his. "I promise to make it up to you."

He looked at her through the bottom of the glass as he took his fill. Rebecca rarely apologised. It had taken some nerve, and she had done it with such poise and sincerity he couldn't help feeling deep admiration and respect for her. He reached over and patted her knee gently, "Apologies accepted, my dear."

She put her glass on the small drinks table, took his cigar and rested it in an ashtray and took his hands and faced him with a smile, "You made a confession earlier about the letter from Timothy and the disclosure of three more grandchildren?"

"I did Rebecca."

"Well – I also – have a confession to make. I, too, received a letter from England, today, addressed to me personally. And it was responsible for making me pull myself together and to stop feeling sorry for myself."

"Was it Marie or Timothy?"

"No,"

Samuel frowned and said: "Do I know this person?"

Rebecca smiled, "Oh, yes, Samuel. You knew this person extremely well."

He sat wracking his brain. After a long pause he said, "I'm sorry. I haven't a clue."

Rebecca viewed him with a teasing smile. "It's none other than your old employer, Lady Claire Hadley!" she declared.

Samuel's mouth opened in astonishment. He was a little nervous at thinking of what Claire actually said in the letter. Had she, for instance, revealed that she and him had been corresponding all these years? Had she also mentioned their daughter Samantha?

Rebecca said, "I'll let you read the letter, later. But basically it's a request for her and me to mend bridges and be reconciled. She feels she's in the twilight of her years, as am I, and we should do it before we go to the grave. She also points out we have both been harmed by the war in the way we have both lost a child to it, her daughter Samantha and my treasured grandson Paul.

She goes on to remind me that she has always held me in the highest esteem. I was regarded as a teacher of merit on the estate. And when we came to Canada, instigated as it had been by the later Squire, she made certain, through her connections, that we would not suffer any hardship." Rebecca paused and said, "And to be fair we never did, Samuel. Did we?"

He shook his head slowly, "No, my dear. And if we did, I caused it when I left the Governor General's Office and went into business with Bill Cornell and we lived in a log cabin with an earth closet and no running water." He hesitated for a moment before he said, " Do you intend to reply to her letter?"

"Oh, yes. I think she deserves a reply. I'll do it in the morning after you have gone off aviating." She invited him to stand and said, "I think it's time for bed. Don't you?"

"What about the dishes?"

"I've plenty of time in the morning."

He threw three large logs on the fire, adjusted the chimney damper and placed the guard in the hearth.

With an arm around each other they climbed the winding staircase. He squeezed her waist and whispered, "You're not, by any chance, wearing those flame red stockings under your dress?"

"I might," she teased him. " Or, there again, I might not."

"And do you still have that net liberty bodice?" he growled

Rebecca did not answer. They reached the landing; she opened the bedroom door and led the way in and hid them from view when she slammed the door shut.

Majorie Towers rose slowly from her night's sleep and took a little while to focus her eyes on the bedside clock. It dawned on her gradually that she had beaten the alarm by nearly two hours, which was most unusual for her. She normally slept right through.

Being a winter morning it was still dark and it was chilly in the unheated bedroom. She pulled the sheet and blankets up around her neck and wallowed in the warmth and comfort of the bedclothes. She puzzled over what had made her awake so prematurely and yet she felt so well and incredibly happy. That also was something of a mystery. She happened to feel one of her breasts and it reminded her that they had become enlarged and felt rather tender in recent weeks. She smiled at recalling how Teddy was always complimenting her on her anatomy, particularly her majestic bosom and her cracking pins, as he described her breasts and legs.

She was pondering on the possible reasons when it occurred to her that she had missed her periods for two months. And on top of all that she had built up quite a big appetite. She had a terrific yen for cheese. All her clothes were beginning to feel tight.

She had put it all down to the physical joy and contentment and intellectual stimulus that Teddy had brought into her life. Then it suddenly came to her out of the darkness on a huge wave of realisation. She sat up in the darkness and reached for her dressing gown that lay upon the counterpane. "I do believe I'm pregnant." she murmured.

She attended school that day in a daze of pride and jubilation. Her colleagues were quick to notice that she more prone to smiling and spoke more gently. Some thought they detected a sparkle in her eyes and a motherly glow lighting her cheeks.

On the way home from school Majorie visited Bessy Parkington the local nurse and midwife. "I wondered if you could spare me a moment, Bessy?"

"Of course, my dear. But I'm due out on my rounds in ten minutes. Step inside."

They moved into a back room and faced one another. Majorie said, "Can I talk to you in confidence, Bessy?"

"That's part of my job."

"I think I'm pregnant. Do you think you could confirm it for me?" And she went on to tell Bessy about the cessation of her periods, her weight gain, her sore and swollen breasts, her appetite for cheese and her tight clothes."

The midwife smiled at her, "It sounds very much like it. And I must say you look very maternal. Good complexion, clear bright eyes, and an appetite for two people are all the symptoms of motherhood." She hesitated and her face darkened when a thought occurred to her. "You haven't come to see me about an abortion, have you?"

"Not at all."

" I apologise for suggesting it but you looked so worried at one point, in the conversation."

Majorie moved to her and held her arms. "You did say you would treat my visit as private and confidential, didn't you?"

"I did, Majorie."

"The point is: the baby, if baby there is, is not the Brigadier's. And I do want to have it. I'm forty years of age and it will probably be my last chance."

"Look," Bessy said picking up her medical bag. "I'll look in on you after my last case on the rounds. Probably be about seven. I'll examine you then."

"Thank you, Bessy. I'd appreciate that."

Majorie, as a result of her visit to the midwife, got home much later than she usually did and was greeted by the frantic yapping of her dog who had been locked in the house all day. As she opened the door the dog did not stop to be greeted by her. It shot between her legs darted up the garden and cocked a leg on the nearest tree and whimpered with relief as it emptied its distended bladder. Majorie put down its food of meat scraps and biscuits, and refilled its water bowl. She took off her shoes; her ankles were swollen. She took off her tight bra and skirt and put on a long sweater and housecoat and busied herself in the kitchen making up a snack of grilled cheese on toast, a pot of tea, and taking it through to the sitting room.

Before sitting down and turning the radio on she looked into the hall, as she did each day, for any mail. She was quite taken aback to see a solitary letter lying on the mat just inside the front door. It was the first one in months. She picked it up, looked at the handwriting and knew, before she opened it, that it was from Gerald, her Brigadier husband.

Ten

On the 15th September they raided Essen.
On the 19th they raided Rostock.
On the 22nd they raided Stuttgart.
On the 29th they raided Berlin.

Wilf Walters had his eye glued to the bombsight and his thumb poised above the tit of the release switch. He felt unusually tense and nervous, lying prone, as he was, in the nose cone that formed the brunt of their attack and at the same time exposed him to the wavering beams of the searchlights, the startling thunder-clapping, exploding shells and the multi-coloured seams of flak. The German capital was well known for being heavily defended. All too often splinters and fragments of shell cases ricocheted off the Perspex nose. He worried that a stray fragment would penetrate the nose and finish him off.

He'd never felt so edgy as he did tonight. He suspected it probably had a lot to do with Majorie's revelation, two days previously, when she proudly told him she was pregnant. She embraced him enthusiastically and thanked him for making it possible. It had the effect of leaving him humbled, yet proud and most certainly it made him mature a little faster and accept the responsibility and dedication that went with the duties of fatherhood.

Of course, always at the back of his mind, was what it would mean to her Brigadier husband. But strangely enough, when he mentioned it to her, it did not seem to bother her. She said he wasn't to worry about it; she accepted full responsibility and would deal with the situation as and when the need arose, using a solicitor if necessary. Although she was confident it wouldn't be necessary.

HC flew up to the target, under his directions, flying the Halifax with the poise and balance of a tightrope walker. A shell exploded nearby and the blast all-but toppled them. The nose veered to the left. He kicked in a bit of right rudder and Walters said:

"Right a bit, skipper – a bit more – that's it. Hold it nice and steady." The beam of a searchlight swept slowly across the nose ahead of them. He wished earnestly that it would go away.

Something exploded overhead and lit up every detail in the Perspex nose cone. He fought down a surge of panic. The target drifted out of the grid wires again. At all costs he mustn't lose his concentration, now. "Left, a bit, skipper – a bit more. Hold it. Steady now." God! Don't let him lose it now, he mumbled into his facemask. Another shell burst overhead and showered the nose cone and cockpit with shrapnel. The sweat began to trickle out of his helmet, run down his face and drip off the end of his mask

"How much longer, Bombs?" HC called.

"Nearly there, skipper. Hold her steady." The Halifax reared up and slewed to the left. "Right- to the right! And get the nose down!" A seam of red flak balls rose up in sight through the grid wires. They reached a height of about fifty feet below the nose, their momentum spent, they arced over and dived back to earth.

The conflagration below that was the target slid to the centre of the grid wires. Walters thumbed the bomb release tit and held it down. "Bombs gone!" he shouted. He lay his head on the sight and closed his eyes in sheer and utter relief.

Presently HC called for the bomb doors to be closed and he opened the engines up to a stricter tempo and they made a long sweeping turn to port. The target passed down their port side a great inferno above which the shells, the flak and the searchlights continued their questing and devastation of a great many of the bombers force that night. Fenny gave the skipper a course to steer for home. And HC ordered Maurice Clarke who he now labeled as Sparks to signal to base that Mission had been accomplished. And the time they left the target.

They overtook a Halifax then another, one with an engine on fire with the flames eating through the engine nacelle and flickering over the wing, and the other pouring thick smoke from an engine. HC did think to contact the two lame ducks but decided against it because there was little he could do to ease their predicament. What was more it was obvious there were Jerry night fighters about?

He took the Halifax on through the night, rolling it gently from side in an attempt to present the aeroplane as a difficult, moving target to any stalking night fighter. Ahead he could see an approaching plain of cloud. He'd feel happier flying above the top of that because he could hop down inside it if trouble threatened.

They were not far from it when there was a big jolt back near the tail and the nose pitched down at an acute angle and a loud scream came over the intercom. It was so shrill and intense the cry pierced through the clamour of the engines. Maurice Clarke felt shivers run up and down his spine, and the hairs on the nape of his neck bristled.

"I'm hit! I'm hit!" Croker shrieked. His rear end and his crutch had suffered a heavy blow when the shock waves and shrapnel from the exploding shell thrust the tail up. He'd never felt such pain before and his groin swelled up to bursting point. Something wet leaked all around the area of his loins and he imagined he was loosing blood. "Someone help me! I'm bleeding to death." he cried and went on wailing and moaning.

HC hauled on the control column to get the nose back up and on to an even keel.

"I think it's rear gun, " Maurice Clarke managed to shout above the screaming cry in his headset. "Want me to go to him, skipper?"

"Thanks, Sparks. And stop that infernal racket he's making by pulling his radio plug out. He'll wake the whole German air force up. Then you plug in and let me know the score"

It took Clarke a good five minutes to get down to the back of the Halifax, groping his way in the dim light of his torch. Squeezing through the narrow opening beneath the wing spar and crouching as he made his way along the narrow catwalk in the cold, metallic shell of the rear fuselage that drummed and echoed to the pounding beat of the engines. Either side of him his torch beam picked out the control cables and the sheathed electrical wiring that serviced the tail unit. It was cold and draughty, he wasn't on oxygen and he was feeling scared of what he might find, or, how he might deal with it. He fell, rose and swayed precariously to the motion of the Halifax. He was suddenly aware that he was without his parachute.

On reaching the turret, he struggled for some time to undo the sliding doors against Davy's weight. He was writhing and waving his arms like a raving lunatic and shouting incoherently at the same time. Maurice traced the radio lead from Davey's flying helmet down to the jacking point, pulled it out and plugged his own in. He tried to shout to the gunner in an attempt to find out what was troubling him. But it was no use; he was hysterical.

"Skipper, Sparks here. He's waving his arms about like a lunatic and won't listen to me. What do I do?"

After a slight pause HC said, "Locate the fire extinguisher in his turret. And give him a sharp tap on the side of the head. It should stun him and give you a chance to see what damage there is to him and the turret."

Maurice located the fire extinguisher and, as directed, gave a sharp blow, to the side of the gunner's helmet. The gunner's flailing arms and legs paused momentarily and his shouting fell to a whimper. But when Clarke tried to move and talk, to him, the hysteria started up all over again.

He gave a sharper blow to the gunner's head, this time, and Croker passed out.

"Skipper this is Sparks."

"Yes, Sparks,"

"I had to use the fire extinguisher twice. Can I have some help to get him out of the turret?"

Fenton offered to go and help and Clarke gave a sigh of relief. He feared again what injuries he might find. And how he would deal with them. He'd never taken his first aid lectures seriously. He wished now that he had.

The navigator came and squeezed past him. He just managed to get his head over the gunner's shoulder and shine the torch inside the turret. Davey was clutching his groin and sat in a pool of dark shiny liquid that he imagined to be blood. It had soaked through his uniform trousers and flying suit. A few inches further back was quite a hole in the turret floor pan and directly above in the Perspex turret roof was a similar hole. It looked as if the cannon shell of a

German night fighter was the culprit. Though the vertical line of entry and exit puzzled him. The fighter must have been climbing or diving vertically. That was not their normal tactics, he was sure.

He got his arms under the gunner's armpits and around his shoulders and hauled his dead weight from the turret. His bulky flying gear got caught a couple of times and he and Clarke made a number of contortions to free him.

They finally carried or, more often, dragged him along the narrow catwalk tense and breathing heavily from their exertions and suffering from lack of oxygen.

They got the gunner propped up against a bulkhead, just forward of the wing spar, hurried around organising oxygen supplies and jacking points for their radio leads and getting hold of a first aid kit. Fenton removed the gunner's helmet to note there was no cut, but quite a swelling, where the extinguisher had hit him. He replaced the helmet and latched the oxygen mask to the face and connected it to a supply. With Clarke holding both the torches he drew the gunner's hands away from his loins to disclose a saturated mass of material that had spread from his groin to his waist. He reached inside the first aid box.

"What are you going to do?" Clarke followed him with the torches.

"There's not much I can do, Maurice. I'm going to give him a shot that'll keep him comatose till we get home. Otherwise he's likely to start flapping his arms again when he comes round."

"Have you ever given an injection before?"

"No. But here's a good time to practice."

"Rather you than me."

Using the scissors from the first aid kit the navigator cut through the leather of the gunner's flying jacket to get at a bare area of arm. He upturned a small phial of antiseptic onto a swab of cotton wool, which he rubbed briskly on the skin. He knelt down and asked Clarke to draw closer with the torches. Holding the arm with one hand he slid the needle in to the skin to a certain depth with the other. Clarke expected it to hurt the wounded gunner. He neither flinched nor batted an eyelid. Fenton thumbed the plunger of the syringe to a certain measure on the glass tube and withdrew the needle. He rubbed the skin once more with the swab and stowed everything back in the first aid box. He got a blanket from the survival pack and draped it over the gunner, particularly over the flooded area of the body.

"We've done about all that could be done." he reported to HC.

"Thanks Peter, thanks Sparks. Oh, and by the way, Sparks. Signal to Beeston that we've got an injured gunner on board. We'll need an ambulance on arrival."

"Will do, skipper."

"And when you've done that, if the rear turret is habitable, you might like to sit and be my eyes to the rear. Should the gun not be working you can just alert me to corkscrew left or right if a Jerry appears on the scene. All right?"

"Understood skipper."

They carried on through the night, and came to the end of the cloud cover making HC feel more exposed. With the clear starlit sky overhead and the dark void below a night fighter could be lurking and waiting to pounce. He kept up his vigilance and maintained his practice of swinging the nose from side to side to confuse any German predator. Fenton came and stood behind him and Edwards and told them they should make their landfall on the Dutch coast in twenty-three minutes. If they looked carefully they could see where the dark Matt texture of the earth ended and the dark gloss of the sea began.

They arrived back at Beeston at three in the morning and Maurice Clarke noticed it was Clarence with a nurse who came in an ambulance to collect Davey. The rear gunner was conscious but rather dazed. They helped him down the ladder and removed his parachute harness, life jacket and helmet which they gave to Maurice. And the last they saw of Croker was him being led up the steps into the ambulance clutching his groin, moaning and groaning to himself.

In the ensuing days Croker was subject to a mixture of ridicule and celebrity status when news of his injuries got on to the gossip of the air force grapevine.

The liquid that he took to be a loss of blood turned out to be hydraulic fluid from a pipeline that operated his turret. A stray piece of shrapnel from the exploding shell, beneath the tail unit, had entered the turret and fractured the pipe causing it to leak onto his crutch. The pain he suffered in his vitals came from the severity of the shock waves released by the shell. He couldn't recall feeling a pain like it before in his life. It made him breathless. The medical officer explained that it could be compared to someone whacking him with a cricket bat. And that it also explained why his organ and appendages had swollen and turned black from the bruising much as any part of the body would when so treated.

For many weeks, much to his embarrassment and unease when in Fiona's company he had to cope with the sniggers and comments about the nature and area of his injuries that somebody had leaked from the Sickbay. He attracted new nicknames of " Longprong" and "Blackballs".

The Squadron officer was in the penultimate position of the conga as it snaked out of the cottage. She held the waist of the figure dancing in front of her and kicked out to the side, with alternate feet. As the Conga made its way down the garden under the starlit sky a figure came from behind her and gripped her thighs and twisted her from side to side to the rhythm of the music that came from a gramophone set near an open window of the cottage. The consumption of two glasses of punch had made her lightheaded and a trifle merry and tempted her to cast off all inhibitions and join the conga.

They reached the bottom of the garden and the leader led them clear of a river and turned to head back up the garden for the cottage. It was at that point that the squadron officer was wrenched away from the chain by the hands gripping her thighs. She was pushed and steered in the opposite direction until she reached the shadows and privacy of an overhanging tree. In her state of inebriation she was rather slow to respond when she was embraced from behind and something nibbled at the lobe of her ear and a male voice whispered, "You're very beautiful and desirable Eunice. And you've been neglected for far too long!"

The senior WAAF officer was both flattered and curious. She could not recall, at any time in her life, a man ever paying her such compliments. And how come he knew her Christian name; she had never divulged it at Beeston. Not even to senior officers. She was flattered by how her phantom admirer pronounced it and spoke so affectionately to her.

Before she could really understand what was happening a pair of deft hands pulled her uniform shirt from the waist of her skirt and travelled swiftly beneath and unhooked and removed her brassiere. It was so quick she did not feel it leave her body.

For a time those searching hands fondled her naked breasts and had them swelling proudly and pointing naked to the stars. More kisses were planted on her neck and throat and more compliments whispered in her ear. It melted the last of any resistance she may have had for his intentions. The stars looked down at her as though shining from a large blue dome. She leant back against him just at the moment the hem of her skirt was raised to her waist and the air breathed cool on the exposure of her body. In one swift, single ripping sound he deprived her of her lower underwear. An arm came across the front of her lower trunk and an arm across her shoulders. In a more gentle movement he bent her forward and took her from the rear.

After some preliminary moments of discomfort he slid comfortably inside her and she went on a journey that was as primitive as it was beautiful, as ravenous as it was delicious, as gratifying as it was passionate. He went deep with his probing and that's when he burst her dam. It gushed from her in a huge wave of relief and a profound satisfaction. She had never experienced anything like it before. It came as a supreme moment in her life. She cried out in celebration as her phantom lover growled heavily in her ear, climaxed, and flourished her with seed.

For a time there was silence. Then she was aware of the gentle but swift movement of his hands as they buttoned her shirt, tucked it in her skirt and pulled the hem of her skirt back to her knees. He whispered his thanks in her ears and was gone. She couldn't remember very clearly what happened after that.

She awoke to a hand gently rocking her shoulder. She opened her eyes to see a hand placing a cup and saucer on her bedside table. "Good morning, marm." her batwoman greeted her.

The senior officer spotted the time on the bedside clock and sat up with a start. "I'm supposed to be taking the church parade this morning! Why didn't you wake me earlier, Mavis?"

"Flight Officer Grace told me to let you lie in as you had rather a late night. She said she would take the parade for you."

"That's all very well. But I'm quite all right."

"You are now, marm. But last night you were quite unsteady, according to flight officer Grace. She managed to get you to take a couple of aspirin before she put you to bed. Otherwise I think you would have had a sore head."

The senior officer thought she saw the batwoman smirking as she turned to leave the room. "Mavis!"

"Yes, marm." She halted.

"What is it you find so amusing. I hope you're not mocking me."

Mavis turned slowly and raised a hand to her face to hide her smile. "The truth is marm is that you have two large red marks on your neck."

The senior officer moved and inspected herself in the mirror of the dressing table. "Where?" she asked..

Mavis pointed nervously to the right side and the back of her neck and used a smaller mirror in conjunction with the larger mirror to clearly show the red welts marking the skin

"What are they, Mavis?"

Mavis said cautiously, "I'd rather leave it to your ADC marm. You might accuse me of insubordination if I tell you."

"They're love bites!" Flight Officer Glade frowned heavily shortly after she arrived back from taking the church parade and told the batwoman to leave the room.

The squadron officer sat motionless, speechless, at the news. She relived the incident at the bottom of the garden. The firm grip on her thighs, those gentle wandering hands, those whispered compliments and that deep and satisfying penetration. She sat before the mirror in something of a daze, floating pleasantly and feeling carefree much as she had after consuming the Punch at the party the other night. Her whole body and mind felt tamed and at ease. Her position in the air force did not seem important anymore. She'd dearly love to know the identity of her phantom lover.

She said to her ADC, "I must confess that I don't remember everything that happened at the party last night."

Flight Officer Glade said, " Half way through the evening I saw you leave the cottage on the end of the conga and go off down the garden. When it came back you were missing. You didn't come back for a good half-hour. I was on the point of coming to search for you when you came in singing to yourself, staggering a little, rather red in the face, your hair disturbed and a whopping big ladder in one of your stockings. You ordered another glass of punch. And then you persisted in asking our host if she had any spare undergarments as you had lost yours in the garden."

"My goodness! Was I that bad?"

"Not altogether bad. You were quite hilarious until you started demanding in a loud voice to know who had stolen your knickers and your bra. It all got a bit embarrassing. So I brought you home and put you to bed." She paused to look at her senior officer. "Did anything happen in the garden, marm, that could compromise your position as senior WAAF officer at Beeston?"

"How do you mean?"

"Well, there might be somebody who has a grudge against you and take any opportunity to get their revenge. A junior male officer you may have upbraided, perhaps, or one of the junior WAAFs who has been up before you for some misdemeanour or whatever."

The senior officer reflected for a moment. Then she roused herself and slapped her knees with both hands. "Well, it's no good crying over spilt milk. I did let myself go. And I confess to having enjoyed it. Yes I would like to know who my lover was, and why he stole my undergarments."

" You mean to say you don't know who it was marm? And that he is actually wandering about with all the evidence he needs to ruin your future in the air force."

"Do you think it's as serious as that?"

"Indeed, I do marm. I think we should make it our business to identify this phantom lover to establish his motives for stealing your underwear. If he chooses to be evasive I suggest you call in the Provos and have him arrested for violation of your person" The Provos being the military police.

"Oh, no. I don't think that would be a good idea at all. It would become public knowledge. And I thought that is what we are trying to avoid."

" Then I suggest we pay a private visit to the cottage and have a chat with the wife of Hadley Chase. It's just possible she has a list of all those who attended the party. And we might deduct from the list, the identity of your phantom lover. In the mean time I'll get Mavis to use her cosmetics to camouflage those bites. I think you should wear your raincoat with the collar turned up when out and about on the station."

Two days later on a cold autumn afternoon they were sat in the small, cosy sitting room of the cottage rented by HC and Jenny. They were seated on the settee whilst Jenny occupied a chair on the right side of hearth in which a log fire crackled and popped merrily and threw its heat into the room. On a small table cups and saucers with silver spoons were laid out attended by a spouted pot covered by a tea cosy and other accoutrements in the form of milk jug and sugar bowl. There were two plates containing sandwiches and biscuits. Occasionally outside the cottage a Halifax roared into the air. It clambered up over the boundary and past the sitting room window, about half a mile away a robust black shape, its undercarriage rising out of sight in the engine nacelles. The urgency of the engine note lessened as the propeller pitch was coarsened and the boost was adjusted for the climb. Others would follow it as the crews took their machines on air test in preparation for a forthcoming operation.

Flight Officer Gale had already outlined the reason for their visit and described the delicate nature of their inquiries.

Jenny said: "Are you saying this so-called phantom lover raped Eunice?"

"Well, yes, in a way."

"No! That's not true." The senior officer interjected. "I never put up any resistance whatsoever. In fact I welcomed his advances and accommodated him in full. He was a real officer and gentleman"

Flight Officer Gale regarded Jenny seriously, "I don't think my senior officer realises the gravity of the situation. If this person were anything of an officer he would have identified himself to her. And if he had respected her he would not have stolen her underwear. He's done that for a reason. To stain her reputation, mark my words. He'll probably send them to OC Beeston or Group stating whom they belong to, treating it as a huge joke. Whereas my commanding officer will be the laughing stock of the WAAFs."

Jenny handed them a cup of tea each and told them to help themselves to the sandwiches and biscuits. She produced a list of all those who had attended the party. And the two officers sat studying it as they sipped their tea and nibbled at the sandwiches.

Jenny said, " I think you could leave out of your suspects all those who brought a partner and just consider any of those who came on their own. Flight lieutenant Harvey Fenton, in my husband's crew, is always on his own, as is flight sergeant Bosanquet. Flight sergeant Priddle, the leader of my husband's ground crew, never brings a partner. And wing commander Herby came to the last party. Nobody was with him. The station Padre popped in for an hour. My husband's squadron commander, Mellows was here. And so was the senior medical officer, squadron leader Buckle."

During the ensuing discussion only the ADC made any attempt to suggest who the suspect phantom lover might be. She thought the gentle hands the voice and the need to remain anonymous pointed to the Padre or the MO. At one point she also considered the ground crew chief might be the culprit. He had bit of a reputation for the ladies, she said. But did not add that he had a fetish for well-built women with a broad beam as portrayed by her senior officer.

Her senior officer would not be drawn. She sat staring into space living in a world of her own. She had done something different with her hair and applied a little rouge and lipstick, Jenny noticed. And she thought Mavis, her batwoman, had done a good job in disguising her love bites.

Jenny also steered clear of making any accusations. She and Peter valued all their guests at the parties they held. What was more she noticed the victim of the incident appeared to be content to let the matter rest? Being an older woman and perhaps denied much of the pleasures and passions in her youth she had probably reached a stage in her life where she thought she was destined for nothing more than her lofty, rather lonely position as a senior air force officer. When the phantom lover took her that starlit night and whispered compliments about her appearance, and his affection for her it had come to her as a distinct pleasure. It breathed into her a dimension of life that had long been denied her. And, now, having savoured it, she hungered for more.

But as of many tragedies and enigmas to spring from the war her phantom lover never did reveal himself, and flight officer Gale never discovered his identity after weeks of discreet inquiries. And neither did the underwear materialise. Eunice attended several other parties at the cottage in the hope she would encounter her phantom lover again. But she never did.

In her own private world she pretended to her family and friends, when she went home on leave, that she had been in a relationship with a member of aircrew who had gone down on a raid.

Eleven

November 29th dawned dull and tranquil at R.A.F. Beeston. There was a good attendance at all the messes for breakfast that morning. The station had been closed the previous evening and notices had been served throughout the station alerting all personnel that a raid was in prospect for the night of the 29th.

Teleprinter messages clattered into the various sections with all the necessary information relating to the raid: the number of aircraft, bomb types and loads to be carried, fuel capacities, weather forecast. Only the nature of the target at this stage was witheld and known only to the most senior officers

The aircrews got down to the dispercals early and fussed around the Halifax bombers with the ground crew preparing the machines for the night's work. Each crew member looked in on his individual domain checking it was neat, tidy and comfortable as it could be for the six, seven or eight hour jaunt they'd be making. Most crews got their aircraft off for a short air test during or after midday. Nobody bothered much about a lunch. They used the mobile NAFFI van to purchase a wad and a mug of tea for refreshment.

When the machines got back down they turned into their dispersal and opened their bomb doors. During the next couple of hours the tractors and bomb trains arrived with a generous supply of HE and incendiaries and loaded each aircraft. And were followed by the big tankers that filled the fuel tanks of each machine.

Edwards and Walters watched it all going aboard in preparation for calculating the all up weight at take-off and determining the centre of gravity where the balance of the Halifax was concerned. Such calculations were not part of Walter's responsibility but Edwards invited him to help because of his mathematical supremacy. They shared the same bedroom in the mess.

When the loading of the bombs and the refuelling was completed the crew were able to board the aircraft again and make their final inspection. The gunners helped the armourers stack the turrets with belts of ammunition. Maurice Clarke checked for the second time that all his radio equipment was working and that he had enough spare valves and condensers. He noted the list of frequencies was readily to hand. On the upper deck behind the pilot's seat Harvey Fenton hummed a little tune. He looked in on his cubby hole whose furnishings comprised of a seat, a plotting table, a porpoise lamp and above the table a single bank of instruments consisting of an airspeed indicator, an altimeter and a gauge that measured the outside air temperature. Unlike the rest of the crew he could enjoy a measure of privacy by closing a dark curtain around the back of his seat. It was really intended to blank him off from distraction whilst he was performing his many calculations as a navigator.

Croker and Clarke got back to their quarters a little after two. Croker stripped down to his vest and underpants and slipped beneath the top blanket of his bed. He lay with his hands behind his head, staring up at the ceiling. He wore a chain and crucifix around his neck and Maurice noticed he had cut back on his smoking in recent weeks. Maurice retrieved an ironing board from behind a wardrobe and set about brushing down and ironing his best blues. And polishing a pair of shoes. After the thrash at the party to celebrate the end of their tour of operations, tomorrow night, he was going home on leave and had arranged for Gloria to go with him. He looked forward to it with a good deal of pleasure.

"Are you going to Liverpool on leave, this time, Davey?" On previous occasions Croker said his hometown was too far away and that he spent more time travelling than being on leave. That's why he didn't bother.

"No," he said. "Fiona wants me to go and meet her parents in Gloucestershire. She's told them we are engaged. And now she wants me to go through the drill of asking her father for her hand in marriage."

Maurice looked askance at him, from his stance at the ironing board, and raised an eyebrow. "Is she from one of those posh families? They do that sort of thing, don't they, getting permission to hitch up with the daughter? Be careful Davey; they'll expect you to be from the officer class and have money behind you!"

Croker said, "Well, Fiona does have class, I'll say that. She speaks well and is very strict on good manners. But from what she tells me, her parents are more religious than well heeled, as they say. They spend most of their spare time in church activities. Fiona is very much like them, you know. She spends a lot of time here in the Station chapel arranging the flowers and helping with the Holy Communion and all that sort of thing."

Maurice said: "Are you sure she has not roped you into all of this against your will. This wearing of the Crucifix and the cut back in your smoking."

"Not really. She doesn't smoke so that makes it a bit difficult. She won't let me kiss her on the lips if I've just had a fag…"

"Less fags more kisses, eh?" Maurice broke in with a chuckle.

"You could say that. But I'll tell you something else, Maurice. I've saved so much money since I cut down on the smoking. I never realised I spent so much."

"What are you going to spend it on?"

"Fiona wants bit of a do when we get married. How would you like to be my best man?"

"What, me!"

"Yes. You, Maurice."

"But I have to give a big speech, don't I? I mean amongst all those big toffs at the wedding. I might forget my words and that would make you look a right monkey."

Croker waved a hand at him, " I'm sure you'd be perfect for the part and I'd like to have you," he said. " Just you think it over on the raid, tonight. And let me know tomorrow."

Maurice finished ironing in the creases of a pair of trousers and hung them on a hanger beneath a tunic on which the brass buttons sparkled. He hooked the hanger on the side of his wardrobe. He'd be going home as something of a hero figure, having completed his tour of ops. And he'd be able to put a crown above his stripes in his promotion to Flight sergeant. My! His mother would be proud. And, now, on top of all that Davy had asked him to be his best man.

He turned to ask Davey, in confidence, what he thought Fiona was like in bed? But he found Davey had turned over in the bed, facing the opposite wall, and had the cover high about his neck and had gone off in search of sleep.

With Walters pedalling, and Edwards on the cross bar, they cycled back to the mess quite some time later than the rest of the crew because they had to wait for the bombs and fuel to go aboard before they could work on the weight and balance calculations. At the mess they used the washroom and made their way to the ante-room, ordered a tray of tea and some lardy cake from a mess steward and managed to get a well-worn leather, easy chair, each, in front of the hearth fire. Over the tea they read whatever newspapers were available. Though Walters was never satisfied unless he could get his hands on a Telegraph and work the Crossword that his lively wit and intelligent expertise could solve in a matter of minutes. He normally did it in eight minutes and concluded his success by draping the newspaper over his face and taking a doze for half an hour.

Edwards forewent any attempts at the crossword. He read the sports pages in the Express and followed his fellow sergeant's example and sought oblivion. It wasn't too difficult after being out in the fresh air for most of the day. The tea and cake and the contrasting heat from the fire quickly induced a relaxed frame of mind and a drowsiness that quickly followed.

HC and Harvey Fenton looked in on the ante room of the officer's mess, found it crowded and decided to go up to the navigator's room after he dropped a pound to a steward to send a tray of tea up to the room. On Harvey's invitation HC took to the easy chair and Harvey used the side of his bed for a seat. Tapping on the door signalled the arrival of the tea. The steward had added a plate of chocolate biscuits. Harvey thanked him and the steward said: "It's the last trip of your tour tonight. Isn't it, sir?"

"The big 30." HC boldly announced.

"Yes, it is Danny." Harvey added.

"Well, I'd like to offer my heartiest congratulations. I remember when you first came to Beeston and flight sergeant Bosanquet was in the crew. He left to take over poor old flight lieutenant Stanton's crew, didn't he?"

"That's right, Danny. And it's also their last op of the tour tonight."

"Oh, so it is. I'd better be off to congratulate them. See you tomorrow night at the big thrash. I can tell you they are preparing something really big."

HC poured and served the tea. He dunked his biscuits in the tea and lost two when they melted and sank to the bottom of the cup. He dug the remains out with a finger.

"So, what do you want to do, Harvey, after we complete the tour?"

The navigator said: "I'm thinking I might apply to be a navigation instructor. The instructional staff were always trying to coerce me when I was training. But I rejected it on the grounds I had had no operational experience to justify taking the job." He grinned. "They gave me some old fashioned looks in response. And it wasn't till then I realised that none of them had been on operations." He paused and said, "What about you Peter? What do you want to do?"

"Find something where I can spend more time with Jenny, or, at least be with her till she has the child. Then do another tour. Let's face it I've only done half this one as captain. Bosey did the first half, didn't he?"

Harvey, forever the loyal, brother officer said, " But you will have flown the thirty ops to qualify Peter. And that's the ruling. If you cast your mind back to just over a year ago aircraft were carrying two pilots and both were credited with a tour of ops after thirty trips together. Just as, in effect, you and Bosey have." He took his uniform top off and stretched out on the bed. "And now it's time for our beauty sleep. I've got a hunch we're going to Berlin tonight." He rolled over on the bed and draped a pillow loosely over his head to blank out the light.

HC removed his jacket and shoes, rested his feet on the bed, covered his chest with the jacket and closed his eyes.

Just after 1700 hours the crews gathered for their pre-op supper whose menu resembled more that of a breakfast of bacon and eggs and tinned plum tomatoes, often referred to as 'red lead' and there were thick slices of bread that others called 'doorsteps' and was spread with thick margarine. The dining hall was filled with that savoury smell of sizzling rashers and fried eggs. All aircrew were each entitled to two eggs. The mugs of tea that followed were a strong, dark brown in colour and hot and sweet to the taste. The munching and crunching continued apace amongst the bubbling conversations and bouts of laughter. WAAF waitresses waited upon them, occasionally having their bottoms pinched by an unseen hand, so fast was the culprit and with so many young men in close proximity it was impossible to decide which one it was. The young women accepted it gamely, as did they when any of the young men remarked on their feminine attributes. They were only too aware that the next time they served supper a lot of these healthy, randy, young men would not have survived tonight's raid.

At 1900 hours the crews, twelve dozen in number, crowded into the briefing hall, considerably more sober and less talkative. The respective briefing officers took their turn on the stand: radio, navigation, armament, engineering, weather and intelligence, each of which gave the relevant information to the crews. The C.O. broke the news that the target was the big B. BERLIN.

HC nudged Harvey Fenton as a reminder of what he had told him that afternoon in his room. Then, Mellows, their Squadron Commander, took to the stage after a word in the ear of Group Captain Swagger.

"Gentlemen, I'd like to say a few words tonight and in particular to the recent newcomers to the squadron. You have, accompanying you tonight, a number of veterans who have been to Berlin on several occasions. And the fact this is their end of tour op tonight is proof that the target is assailable despite all the nasty tales and rumours you have heard about Berlin and its impenetrable defences. Flight Sergeant Bosanquet, amongst you, is on his fourth tour of ops and, I understand, this will be his thirtieth visit to Berlin, tonight."

"Give him thirty Berlin medals, then!" somebody shouted.

Mellows grinned and said, "You also have flying officer Hooper with you who has survived twelve visits to Berlin." He smiled. "I'm not saying he always got back in one piece. He came back on one occasion with an engine missing. They say he sold it to the Germans for one of their Dorniers."

"Give him an Iron Cross!" another voice shouted from the crowd.

Mellows allowed the ensuing laughter to subside and said, "Flight Lieutenant Hawker not only has been to the capital several times but his gunners disposed of six Jerry night fighters on such raids. And, finally, we have Flying Officer Hadley-Chase and Sergeant Brent who are also veterans when it comes to visiting the Big B. So I can assure you gentleman you are in good company. I wish you all every success and a safe return. Thank you and goodnight. See you over Berlin."

From way across the room a voice shouted. "You didn't mention Sergeant Croker, sir. He went to Berlin. And he came back with black balls!"

The room erupted into laughter, shared as it was by the group of officers lining the stage. At first the gunner was tempted to cringe. Then Clarke and Walters manhandled him onto a tabletop and forced him to take a bow. The amusement and laughter did much to ease the pre-op tension and distract thoughts from the dislike and fears of the target.

They filed out of the hall and went to the locker room to dress for the flight. The room thrummed to the babble of voices. There was a strong drift of serge and wool, and leather and fleece as they dressed. Silk inner socks and woolen outer socks. Inner flying suits and kapok outers. Long woolen roll neck sweaters. Silk gloves and leather gloves. Leather, fleece lined jackets. Helmets and goggles. Heavy suede flying boots.

A number of the crews wore their own scarves, some retained from their school days, others knitted by a girlfriend or a Woman's Institute eager to make their contribution to the War Effort and provide a little comfort for the daring, young flying warriors of the night.

Gradually they made their way to the other hall that accommodated the safety equipment. They bundled themselves into life jackets, popularly known as Mae West, over which they arranged a parachute harness. They were also issued with a parachute, torches, thermos flasks of coffee and Benzedrine tablets. But Bosey and HC never encouraged their crew to take the latter. They contended that if any of the crew couldn't stay awake for an operation they should pack up flying. And they also maintained that the hangover, after the effects of the drug wore off, was more severe and painful than that suffered after drinking too much grog.

Croker adjusted his position in the queue so that Fiona would serve him with his gear. She pushed his pile of kit across the counter and stealthily touched his hand. And when he signed for the kit he removed a folded piece of paper from beneath the Crocodile clip at the top of her board. "Have a nice trip, David" she whispered. He looked quickly at her and mimed his thanks. He couldn't wait to get to the aircraft to read her note in private.

Mellows led the way outside and they clambered into the queue of trucks that would ferry them to the dispersed aircraft. The moon was up and the air had a chilled feel about it. When they arrived at D-Dog the ground crew were loitering and their chief got HC to sign the form 700. Harvey Fenton tallied by the truck awhile and invited the WAAF driver to take a couple of boiled sweets from a paper bag he was holding. It was something he'd started up since HC took over the captaincy of the crew. He considered it as a tip and a gesture of goodwill to a member of ground staff.

HC saw Croker to his rear turret, a ritual he had picked up from Bosey.

Croker climbed into the hatch and turned, "Thanks skipper."

In the darkness HC said, "By the way, I've recommended you have a crown attached to your stripes. By tomorrow night you'll be a flight sergeant."

"Thanks, skipper. Thanks a lot." And he was gone, crawling to the rear turret.

HC checked the hatch was flush and secure and walked around the Halifax to the front crew hatch and climbed up inside to join the others. The confined space of the cockpit reeked of cold metal, aircraft paint, engine fuel, engine oil, grease, his leather helmet and the rubbery smell of his oxygen mask. He settled himself in his seat and checked its height, and its distance from the control column and rudder pedals, and that the engine controls were within reach. Edwards moved beside him going through the starting checks, getting the electrical circuits buzzing with current, the fuel gurgling through the lines and priming the engines and setting the engine controls. "All set for starting, skipper," he called.

HC shouted through the side vision vent, "Ready to start port inner?"

"All clear," a voice shouted back from the ground. "Contact port inner!"

One moment the Halifax was still and lifeless. In the next moment it was shuddering as the propeller turned over, gathering speed. HC flicked the magneto switches on – and the engine crackled into life. And whilst he checked the readings on the oil pressure and oil temperature and cylinder head temperature gauges, Edwards bawled out of his window for clearance to start the starboard inner. The noise grew louder, the vibration stronger and both intensified when the other two engines were brought to life. It lessened a little when they closed the side vents.

"Captain to crew, Radio check. How goes it Bombs?"

" All clear, skipper."

"How's it with you Sparks?"
"Loud and clear, skipper."
"All okay your end, navigator?"
"All tickety-boo, captain."
"Can you hear me Rear Gun?"
"Very well. Thank you, skipper."

"Right! Let's go." He released the brakes, gave a burst of power to the two inner engines and let the Halifax gather some way before applying the brakes. The heavily loaded machine waddled to a halt. They continued off the grass and joined the perimeter track leading to the runway and he called out the take-off checks to Edwards as they went. They set the elevator, aileron and rudder trimmers. They ensured the four engine mixture controls were in the fully RICH position. They did likewise to the four propeller pitch levers and noted they were in the fully FINE position. They checked all the fuel cock positions, pressures and the contents. They put the flaps down ten degrees, told the rest of the crew to check their hatches and harnesses. HC noted all the gyro instruments were working and set the directional gyro to read the heading of the liquid compass. He just had time to check the controls for full, free and correct movement before they reached the queue at the runway. Whilst waiting their turn HC got the first course to steer from Harvey. It came as course MAGNETIC and the pilot had to consult the compass deviation card in order to arrive at course COMPASS before it could be set on the compass.

At last their turn came to take-off. "Captain to crew. Here we go!" He pushed the throttles up the quadrant. Edwards mounted guard with his left hand. The crackling engines opened out to a growl and, at full power to a ferocious roar. The noise in the fuselage reached its peak and, at first, it was quite disproportionate to the acceleration of the lumbering bomber. HC pushed the control wheel forward to get the tail up. And then she improved upon her ambling gate. She surged forward and careered over the ridge midway of the runway and accelerated down the slope on the other side. It always looked as if they would never clear the boundary fence and hedgerows. However, at nighttime, you couldn't see it so well and therefore it was less alarming. "90knots." Edwards called.

HC gave it another 5knots and hauled back on the control wheel. She staggered into the air, dropping the left wing a bit but which he corrected with a dash of right rudder. He eased the back pressure on the wheel and she picked up a bit more speed, which he used to bank them to the left and fly out over the cottage where he waggled the wings in farewell to Jenny. She said she often stood outside to watch a raid go out. But he didn't see her tonight. He got busy climbing on course.

Walters grinned to himself. He had spotted Majorie's cottage just way down to the right just as they lifted into the air and a little before HC banked to the left. He thought of her and the things that had passed between them down there in that tiny home. He thought of the child she was expecting. She had started a bottom drawer and had shown him the baby clothes she was collecting and making. She had knitted little cardigans and leggings and booties. She was currently making linen dresses from paper patterns bought from a haberdashery. He regularly thought of her husband languishing in the far off prison camp and it gave him a conscience.

He thought that if she divorced the Brigadier and married him it might make everything more legal, more clean and tidy. But Majorie never agreed with him each time he brought the matter up. She repeatedly said they must cross that bridge when they got to it.

"My dear, dear Teddy please try and understand my position. What is the point of divorcing Gerald, now? He might not survive the time in the POW camp. In which case my marriage would be automatically annulled. And," she held the airman's hands and looked searchingly into his eyes. "What if I did marry you? And the war claimed you. How do you think I'd stand then? One has to be practical, Teddy."

He couldn't bring himself to ask her how he would stand if and when her husband came back on the scene. The way he saw it she wanted to have both her cake and eat it.

"Navigator to Wireless." Harvey Fenton cut in on his thoughts.

"Yes, navigator?" replied Maurice Clarke.

"Can you get me a radio fix on Beeston and Charlton. Then I'll get the exact spot where we landfall the coast. You, Wilf, get me a visual, if you can."

"That won't be difficult," Walters told him. "With the full moon it's nearly bright as day."

Edwards, sat alongside HC, scanned all the engine instruments to satisfy himself and the Skipper that all the engines were behaving themselves and it was safe to carry on with the operation. He nudged one of the propeller pitch levers forward to synchronise the revs of the engine with its three companions. There had been the slightest hint of a hunting note in the overall roar of the engines. Only the fine-tuning of his hearing as a conscientious engineer could have detected it.

He slouched a little on his seat; he was feeling incredibly weary and had been like it for weeks. He found it increasingly difficult to stay awake for an entire operation. And to be honest with himself he was like it on the ground. It had all started when he got serious with Joyce. She had an insatiable appetite for making love and gorged on him every time they met whereas, sometimes, he would have liked a change and a break from it. He had come to the conclusion that she was draining him dry physically and mentally and that if he didn't do anything about it he'd end up as a nervous wreck. His eyes were permanently sore and enflamed; his eyeballs felt they were bulging and resting on his cheeks.

He had decided that when he went on leave in the next two or three days he wouldn't tell her. He desperately needed a break from her to get some rest and nourishment to get his strength back. He was sure his mum's cooking; her steak and kidney pies and greens, and her plum duff puddings and custard would do the trick.

"Like to take a spell back at your console, Engines?" HC called over the R/T and nudged him. "You've got a better seat back there."

Edwards thanked him and made his way aft, smiling. It was if the skipper had been reading his mind. In the darkness and surrounding beat of the engines he took a fill of coffee from his thermos and it revived him a little.

"Sparks to Navigator. Beeston 270 degrees. Charlton 225 degrees."

The navigator plotted the bearings on his Mercator's chart. And the lines intersected at a point right on the edge of the Wash. He was about to ask Wilf if he could get a visual when the Bombaimer announced they were crossing the coast at that moment. Harvey made a note of the time on his log.

"Captain to rear gun. Everything all right back there?"

"Yes. Thank you skipper. There are a lot of aeroplanes following us. You can see the moon shining on the windscreens and the turrets."

"Good show! Let me know if they get too close."

"Will do, skipper." Croker replied. He felt warm, comfortable, cheerful and calm. His life had changed so much since Fiona had become part of it. She had a nice, gentle way of encouraging him to better himself and to see the best in people. She set a good example by the way she spoke, the way she behaved and in her reverence for the Church. It was her who had presented him with the gold chain and crucifix. And he treasured it. It was her who got him to look at the skipper in a different light and refrain from putting people in classes. Yes – there were rich and poor people, she admitted. And there were those who had the better chance of an education and sometimes remained aloof from their less fortunate brethren. But these people deluded themselves by thinking they were superior, she explained. Because when it came down to it they only had one head, two eyes, a nose a mouth, two arms and legs, and a heart just as any other mortal. She said it was people like him who were just as guilty of creating class barriers and she described it as inverted snobbery.

In the station chapel one Sunday she drew his attention to the great difference in ranks among the congregation. There was two wing commanders, three squadron leaders, a couple of, flight lieutenants, half a dozen pilot officers, perhaps a dozen NCOs, and the equivalent in airmen. And in not so quite big numbers were officers and lower ranks of the WAAF. The station padre was a squadron leader. "There's no rank in here, David," she whispered in his ear. "Everyone, including you, holds the humble title of, Christian."

He smiled beneath his mask as he looked at the great armada of dark winged shapes following him, gently wavering and rising and falling. He liked to think that in years to come when he and Fiona had produced a family he'd sit by the fireside and tell them of his adventures in the war.

"Navigator to pilot. Change course forty five degrees to port onto zero eight zero."

"Roger, navigator. Zero eight zero degrees."

They weren't that far from the target, Croker remembered from the briefing. The course change took them off the heading for Berlin in order to hoodwink the Germans into thinking the bomber force was heading for a target other than the German capital. The moon glinted on the bombers as they changed course. D-Dog shuddered for a time as it hit the prop wash from a Halifax ahead of it.

Then the disturbed air reached the tail unit and Croker heard it on either side of him buffeting the tail plane. It lasted only a matter of seconds and it was gone.

They flew on for another forty minutes then, "Navigator to pilot. Change course to one eight zero degrees. Estimating target in twenty three minutes."

"Roger, navigator, one eight zero degrees."

The lead aircraft led them around on a fairly tight turn and they swept toward the target. Eight minutes from the target the curtains of the night drew apart and the footlights of the stage, in the form of searchlights, beamed up in clusters. The booming sound of big bass drums, from an unseen orchestra, struck at the sky and coloured balls of light rose in high lobs, and unhindered, fell over in an arc and returned to earth. For a time the four thousand engines of the raiders dominated the sky. Then to the left and right of the scene there were muffled explosions and great sheets of light as an accurately placed shell or a deadly seam of flak downed a machine.

Smaller winged shapes joined the affray. Night fighters! Someone called over the R/T. The fighters flew amongst the bomber stream having a huge choice of victims to pick from. In the madness and confusion of the moment bombers collided with each other. Bombs falling from aircraft above them hit some of their number. The flashes and explosions became more frequent, more devastating. The German ground defences fought desperately to bring justice to the aerial raiders; they threw anything that was possible to throw into the air to stem the flow. But the more they dispelled or brought down, the more, it seemed, were available to fly in and fill the gap.

Suddenly amongst the noise, the carnage, chaos and the high drama someone left a radio transmit button or switch on and into the headsets of every crew member, of every surviving aircraft came a deeply moving and inspiring male voice that quoted lines from Shakespeare's King Henry the Fifth:

> Once more unto the breach, dear friends,
> once more;
> Or close the wall up with our English,
> dead!
> In peace there's nothing so becomes a man
> As modest stillness and humility:
> But when the blast of war blows in our ears,
> Then imitate the action of the tiger;
> Stiffen the sinews; summon up the blood,
> Disguise fair nature with hard-favour'd rage;
> Then lend the eye a terrible aspect.

Walters was lying in the nose with his eye glued to the bombsight when a succession of clumping noises crashed up through the floor before him. The Perspex nose cone shattered, a great rush of freezing cold air came in at him. The nose tilted down and he was thrown forward. He tried to treat it as a joke as he lay hanging precariously over the jagged remains of the nose section, looking down into the void at a distant cluster of fires. Any second now he was going to be thrown helplessly over the edge without being able to reach back for his parachute, such was the force of the dive. The air roared at him and it was getting very cold. Another seam of flak, from the German ground defences, crashed through the floor and exploded – the force deafened him, he felt a blow on the side of his head and was dazzled by a great white flash before his eyes. Suddenly he was free of the Halifax and he floated in space. He had a strange sensation of drifting amongst the stars, and beneath him he could clearly see fields and rivers and trees and hills in the flooding light of the moon. My, oh my! It gave him an incredible feeling. Within him, and without, everything was so tranquil, so untroubled, so unhurried. He saw Majorie waving up at him, smiling. She looked so young and beautiful. He waved gaily back at her and continued on his ethereal journey…

"Bombs! Do you read me?" HC called as he struggled to recover the Halifax from the dive. He called again and got no answer.

"Skipper this is Sparks." Clarke cried. "You won't get him. He fell out of the nose. And he didn't have his parachute. I couldn't reach him. I'm sorry skipper."

"All right, Sparks, I'm sure you did your best. Now! Is your radio operating?"

"Yes, sir."

"Right. Signal Beeston and tell them we've lost the bombaimer. Then come to the top deck. It must be getting a bit draughty down there. I can feel it coming up here."

When the wireless operator reached the top deck he was numb and in shock from Walter's departure from the aircraft without a parachute. Fenny seated him at his chart table and gave him a thermos top of coffee.

"Captain to crew. I intend to clear the target and head for home. I may have to take a lot of evasive action to clear this lot. So be prepared."

They never did see or hear what hit them.

Bosey was following them up to the target when he saw the Halifax lurch and stagger when the flak balls did their deadly deed and took the nose cone off. From what he saw, Peter got it under control and started to take evasive action. In the moonlight the Halifax sideslipped down to the left. It was about to swing back and sideslip down to the right when it exploded with a muffled roar and a startling flash that even took Bosey unaware.

It did not blind him because he had his tinted goggles pulled down. But he was shocked at the violent suddenness and finality of it all. First there was the dark form of the Halifax. Then in a fraction of a second of the explosion; the port wing snapped off and flew upwards and, at the same time the starboard wing and engines simply parted company with the fuselage and fell earthwards. The fragmented remains of the Halifax hung for a moment in the fading light of the explosion before showering to earth. He found himself shouting out, "Oh, no!" Because it occurred to him that amongst all those tiny fragments there surely must be what had once been his stepbrother Peter, and Harvey Fenton, and Wilf Walters, young Maurice Clarke and Edwards and Davey Croker. It seemed incredible, impossible in fact, that they could be whisked away from life and reduced to splinters of bone and pulped, dissolving flesh. He hauled on the control wheel and footed on some rudder to get the Halifax around to starboard to avoid flying into the exploding debris. But just when he thought he was drawing level with the remains of M-Mother there was nothing but a blank space. The remains were already showering earthwards. He happened to look down between the fuselage and the port inner engine and saw down in the depths a flickering ball of fire growing smaller. To eventually disappear amongst the fire-ravaged earth that was Berlin.

"Corkscrew left, skipper!" It was his tail gunner. "Make it quick. It's a night fighter."

Bosey threw himself on the control column and kicked in a bit of rudder. German night fighters didn't normally operate over the target. But he should have known better; this after all was the big B, the German capital. The lumbering Halifax rolled and yawed, first in one direction then the other. Back at the tail the four Brownings rattled and stammered as they spat into the night sky at the pursuing German.

"I think I got him!" the gunner shouted jubilantly.

Bosey was corkscrewing right when he saw a silhouette pulling up to his left trailing a long plume of flame. Its momentum spent the German fell over like a Catherine wheel and descended from the scene, the plume changing from white and green to an orange and red colour.

Moments later he saw a bright flash as it struck ground.

"Well done rear gunner. I think I can confirm that one for you."

"Thanks skipper."

"Bombaimer to skipper. Are we? Or are we not? Going to do a bomb run. We've nearly overrun the target." The voice was tense, impatient.

Bosey said: "I'm not going around for another try with all these fighters about, if that's what you think. I'll open the bomb doors and she's all yours. Aim straight ahead and get the bombs away as soon as possible and before another Jerry fighter takes a swipe at us." The violent, instantaneous destruction of Peter's Halifax had impaled itself on his memory and his emotions. His thoughts raced about in all directions. In the mind's eye he kept seeing the flash and the exploding pieces of D-Dog and couldn't fully comprehend it. It just didn't seem possible that so huge an aeroplane, and all those characters who made up the crew, and who he knew personally, could be snatched from life in a margin of time that could be measured by the blink of an eyelid.

"Bombs gone!" shouted Sharpe, his bombaimer.

He roused himself and told his engineer to get the bomb doors closed. He opened the throttles, pulled the nose up and kicked on left rudder. The Halifax hesitated for a moment then rolled over, and they all-but went onto their backs as it reached over and went diving down and around the target on a reciprocal heading, and started on the long jaunt back to Beeston.

In the operations room at Beeston the girls wrote the aircraft movements up on a wall-length blackboard. Two of their number sat before a telephone, another two worked on the end column chalking in each of the machines as they arrived back at Beeston. Twenty- four machines had set out on the raid, two had aborted because of technical problems, and five had not reported leaving the target. In the last few minutes five had landed and seven were in the circuit and queuing up to land. That meant another five were unaccounted for.

Wing Commander Herby was in attendance primarily to greet his two sons and congratulate them on completing their tour of operations. He was in no doubt what it would mean to their ageing grandfather in Canada when he got wind of it. Peter will have completed his first tour and Jaque will have completed his fourth. He stirred at seeing Jaque's call sign, M-Mother, entered in the 'Arrivals' slot. He frowned at Peter's call sign, D-Dog. The only entry in the line was the time he set course from Beeston. He approached one of the girls sat before a telephone. "Are you sure you've not had any messages from D-Dog?" he said.

"Not on this line, sir. You might go next door and check if W/T has received anything."

He did as she suggested and the WAAF sergeant, got each of her girls who sat before a radio console, wearing earphones which enabled them to track transmissions from any of the aircraft , to scan through their message pads for any signals from D-Dog.

There weren't any, he was told. He went back to the other room spurred by the sound of a telephone ringing for attention. He hurried back just as a girl snatched up the receiver. She listened for a moment or two then called to one of her colleagues working on the blackboard, "B-Baker and T-Tommy, landed." And it was entered against the two call signs in chalk in the end column.

Shortly after, the telephone girl announced that M-Mother had landed. The Wing Commander waited for her to confirm Q-Queenie and R-Robert had landed and decided to make his way to the debriefing hall. Crews were sat around tables confronted by an intelligence officer. And he overheard comments of: "It was bloody!" "It was a hell hole. Kites going down all over the place." "There were scores of deadly night fighters." "People were banging into each other." "The flak was murderous and the shells were more accurate than ever before." "The searchlights – I've never seen so many bloody searchlights!" the clamour of voices continued and rose and fell and the air grew more foggy with cigarette smoke.

Herby saw his son Jaque and his crew enter the room grim-faced, strained. It must have been bad as so many of them were saying. He headed for his son and as he passed a table a comment obviously meant to reach his ears said, "It's time for big daddy H and his bigwigs to go to Berlin and see how bad it is. It's a suicide run and make no mistake about it."

He moved on and met his son. "A bad one, was it?"

Bosey grinned at him, his face lined and creased by the edging of his flying helmet and oxygen mask. "Well, let me put it this way: It certainly was not: 'A piece of cake'."

"Have you heard anything of Peter?"

Bosey told his crew to get a table and that he'd join them presently. He led the wing commander to a quiet spot. "Peter will not be coming back, Pops."

"You mean he..." He couldn't bring himself to say the word.

"I saw it. It was a direct hit."

"Where was he? And what was he doing?"

"They were running up to the target. And for some unknown reason they started taking evasive action. They might have picked up some flak or a fighter got at them. I don't know. But I'm fairly certain it was an accurately placed shell that finished them off." He paused and added, " They should not have been on the raid tonight if the truth be known. That's what makes it so galling."

The wing commander frowned heavily and said, "Whatever do you mean?"

Bosey said, "This was their thirty first operation tonight. Early in the tour when I was with them, there was a recall shortly after we got airborne due to duff weather. But Peter decided to press on and Harvey Fenton, his navigator, and I agreed. We went through some atrocious weather and reached the target, dropped our eggs and came back home. It counted as an operation as far as I was concerned."

"But, of course. When did you first twig the oversight?"

"Shortly after Peter went down and I was heading for home. It's my fault really; I should have spotted it before we went on the raid."

The wing commander patted him on the back. "Well you mustn't hold it against yourself. Put it down to fate. And look at it this way: you also did one operation over the top and you survived. That's fate also." He motioned to Bosey's crew who was waiting for him to join the debriefing. "We'll meet up again after you have finished."

Bosey said, "Would you like me to break the news to Jenny?"

"No, my boy. We'll go together."

Majorie Towers had been awake for most of the night. She stayed up to watch the raid set out. From her garden she saw the big lumbering black shapes of the roaring Halifax bombers rise up from the unseen aerodrome and climb up past the cottage, a small light glowing at the extremity of the wings and the tail and small flames spurting from all four of the engines. They came in a stream; each separated by a couple of minutes. She thought she counted twenty- four of them. They made a wide climbing turn through a hundred and eighty degrees and headed east still climbing. They slowly faded into the darkness of the night, as did the sound of their engines.

She stood a little longer enjoying the tranquility and admiring the moon and the stars. It was a beautiful night, rather chilly perhaps, but each time she thought of Teddy and the child, she was expecting, she felt a positive glow of pride. She blew a kiss to the sky in the direction he had gone and returned indoors. She made a mug of Ovaltine and took it to bed and read a book for a spell before sleep claimed her.

She awoke with a start, looking up at the dark ceiling. And the little treasure in her womb was kicking like mad. She'd been dreaming but couldn't remember what it was about. She got up, trod into her slippers, put on a dressing gown and went to the kitchen and warmed some milk in a pot and poured it in a glass. She took it to the settee in the sitting room and sat pondering. The dream came back to her slowly: there was a great crashing noise and then she was falling – falling – falling. In desperation she reached out and called for Teddy to help her. Suddenly he was there dressed in all his flying gear. He held her hand and slowed her descent and lowered her gently to the ground. She turned to thank him but he was already rising away from her. Then he said something most odd "I can't stay, Eunice," he called down to her. "But I'll always be near if you need me."

She waved and beamed a smile back up at him. "You promise, Teddy? You promise?"

"I promise, Eunice." And he disappeared from view.

That was when she awoke from the dream.

An unknown source compelled her to get off the settee and go and look outside the cottage. As she did so she witnessed a shooting star streaking through the constellations. It had a long tail and lasted all of twelve seconds before it burnt itself out. It was the second one she had ever seen in her life; the first was many years ago and she remembered her grandmother saying it signified a death.

By this time she was too alert to go back to bed. She prodded the fire into life and banked it up with a couple of logs, brought a table lamp to bear near the arm of her favourite easy chair and delved into her knitting bag. As she worked the needles her mind went back to the kicking in her womb. She smiled; it had been so full of life. Life that she had helped to create. It made her feel infinitely proud. What a pity her parents were not alive to see their grandchild; they were always on about it when she and Gerald first got married. What would they have thought had they known he wasn't the father?

Her mind switched back to the kicking again and she remembered the midwife remarking that early movement in the womb pointed to a girl. Boys, she said, tended to be lazy. With this in mind Majorie began to debate what she would call the girl. In the beginning she rather hoped it would be a boy and had discussed with Teddy the name of Gareth after his Welsh origins. Now, she hit on the name of Willamena and thought it quaint but apt for a girl who came from quality parents.

Round about three in the morning the floor of the cottage began to hum quietly like a generator and the roof echoed to the distant pounding beat of the engines of the returning bombers. Unlike the outward flight they came back in dribs and drabs, engines throttled back. They joined the aerodrome circuit, flying around the back of her cottage and creeping around the front where she could watch their dark shapes outlined by the glowing wingtip and tail lights, the spluttering exhaust plumes and dangling undercarriages. With the moon resting lower in the sky they weren't so visible. She went and fetched an overcoat and put on a pair of socks. The fading moonlight just managed to show a glistening layer of frost on the shrubbery and small lawn in the garden, and on the felt roof of her potting shed. She counted the ninth Halifax to go around the cottage and make its way onto the downwind leg. A pause of something like five minutes and another two let down over the cottage. Then there was a break of something like ten minutes before another one arrived.

She waited another ten minutes, but no more arrived and the night fell silent. She went back inside and warmed herself by the fire. Surely they had not lost twelve aircraft on the raid? Because that's what she made it, having counted them set out and counted them when they returned. She listened intently hoping to detect more coming back. But there was not a sound.

She reverted back to the knitting and in a few minutes she nodded off in the chair. She came to again at eight in the morning and hurried around washing and getting dressed driven by her personal discipline that told her a woman of her age and a mother-to-be should not be lounging about in bed at so late an hour in the morning.

At nine o'clock Flight Sergeant Bosanquet and Wing Commander Herby arrived at the door of her home.

Fiona stood at the counter in the safety section receiving back the equipment from the crews. She quickly looked over the parachute packs and harnesses and life jackets for damage and soiling and put the affected ones to one side. She also briefly inspected the torches and thermos flasks and put them in the respective racks and pigeonholes. The queue of men arriving was not large. They came in twos and threes and without exception they all looked pale, drawn and solemn, indicating that the raid had not been successful. They were far from buoyant in their conversation and she knew from experience not to press them. Most of them had a cigarette dangling from their lips. She looked frequently toward the double doors, where they all came in, hoping to catch sight of anyone from D-Dog.

Eventually the place was empty and quiet. She whiled her time away using a cloth and a cleansing agent to clean the webbing of a number of parachute harnesses and life jackets. She got a young woman of junior rank to wash and sterilise the thermos flasks.

They were on the verge of completing the work when Flight Lieutenant Rawlings, her section leader, called her to his office. She approached the office quite certain that he would tell her of the losses of safety equipment that night and how many replacements she needed to order in the morning. But as she got to the door she noticed Bosey lingering inside. On seeing her enter Rawlings made an excuse to leave and said the pilot wanted to speak to her in private. Her heart turned over and a strange tingling feeling went up and down her spine and made her hair stand on end.

"I regret he won't be coming back, Fiona," he gripped her gently by the arms. "In fact none of D-Dog will."

"Oh, my God!" she threw herself against him. And he wrapped his arms around her. She smelt the serge of his uniform and fought back the tears; she must set the example of no dramatics and exhibit a stiff upper lip; she wasn't the only one in grief tonight she told herself. She drew a deep breath and eased away from him and used a hanky to wipe her moist eyes. "How many did we lose tonight, Bosey?"

He gave her a cigarette and lit it for her. "At the moment ten aircraft are missing. So that means some sixty aircrew. But we have yet to find out if any of them landed elsewhere. Or if they went down in Germany and were taken prisoner."

She said quickly, "Is it possible that David and the others are among them?"

"No, I'm afraid not. They got a direct hit on the run up to the target. I saw it happen. I wasn't far behind them." He paused and added, "We also lost squadron leader Mellows and flight lieutenant Hawker tonight."

"Goodness, gracious! I've known them from the beginning; they're veterans like you." She hesitated and said, "What about flying officer Hooper and Sergeant Kent?"

"They got back all right," he grinned and said, "Forgive me for laughing but Tony Hooper is still bleating about his inadequate Halifax. I heard him complaining at the debriefing. Do you know that Halifax completed its second tour of ops tonight."

Fiona smiled and said, "For several weeks he complained that the crutch of his parachute harness was too tight. Until one of our girls told him to stop bragging. We never heard another word from him."

Bosey grinned and stirred. "Would you like me to walk you back to your quarters?"

"Thanks, Bosey. But I'll be all right. By the way will you be telling Jenny?"

"I'm going over later with Wing Commander Herby. We'll also call in on Wilf Walter's friend. Eunice, isn't it?"

"Yes. Painful though it is, I think she'll appreciate a visit from you."

Fiona wandered back to her quarters; the moon had set but the stars remained sharp and clearly twinkling. A harsh ground frost glistened on the tarmac of the road, upon which she walked, and as she approached another gathering of buildings she noticed the apex roofs were coated likewise. After a time she felt its icy bite nipping at the lobes of her ears and making her nose run.

The contrasting warmth of her quarters made her face glow. She undressed to her slip and rinsed her face and hands. And with the framed photograph of David looking at her from the top of her bedside cabinet she knelt by her bed, hands clasped, and immersed herself in prayer.

Twelve

It was a little after midday when the telegram boy arrived at the Fentons' residence to
find that nobody were at the house He, doubtfully, pushed a small yellow envelope through the letterbox of their front door; he was supposed to deliver the message personally and wait for a reply.

Jim Fenton had reported for work at the usual time that morning. By lunchtime he was in the company sick bay asking for a remedy. He felt cold, lethargic and heady. It had started during the middle of the night when he awoke from a dream whose details he could scarcely remember but which had left him weak and shivery. It reminded him of the one and only bout of influenza he had suffered in his life and occurred around the time Harvey's sister was stillborn. The company nurse gave him a course of tablets, a sick note, and told him to take three days off.

He put his motorcycle inside the garage alongside his car that rarely saw the roads, in these days of petrol rationing. He moved in the back door of the house, got a kettle on the gas ring to make tea, and put a match to the fire in the sitting room. It would make a pleasant surprise for Mary to come home to a warm house for a change. A little later he was moving into the hallway that led upstairs from the sitting room when he spotted the yellow envelope laying forlornly on the inside mat of the front door. The paper communication took on a spine-chilling rather unwelcome significance in time of war. It rarely brought good news or happiness.

Jim had always accepted that Harvey was at risk as a navigator in bomber command. Information reaching Vickers showed that the losses in terms of aircraft and crews had reached such a critical stage at one point in the war that all operations were transferred from day to night. Had they not done so there was every chance the twin-engine element of bomber command would have been wiped out. And such were the concerns when the larger, four engine bombers came on stream their losses were only kept to a minimum by operating at night. Jim could not bring himself to open the envelope. He left it propped up against the clock on the mantelpiece, in the sitting room. He poured the tea and sat before the growing warmth of the fire, enjoying a pipeful of tobacco. He knew he could put forward a number of reasons to explain how he would cope with the loss of his son. His dilemma would be breaking the news to, and coping with, Mary. He began to dread the moment she was due home. And the first question she routinely asked each day, when arriving home from work, was, "Any mail from Harvey?"

Some three hours later and sixty miles away in a brick terraced council house the Clark family were sitting down to a cooked tea of bangers and mash and baked beans, which would be followed by junket, lardy cake and mugs of strong sweet tea. Bella and Billy had a tendency to gulp their food and their father was constantly reminding them about it. He attributed it to bad manners rather than that they were young and had healthy appetites. "A bit of military service like our Maurice, would do you two a world of good." he snapped.

Mrs Clark did not always agree with her husband's chastising of the children. But she never interfered. She looked at Maurice smiling out from a photograph on the dresser. She thought he looked rather important in his air force blue uniform on which he proudly wore his air gunner's single wing brevet. She was very proud of him.

As a child he had been slow and ponderous destined, as she often thought, for nothing big in life. In her motherly way she had concentrated on building on his strengths which were politeness and his ability to get on with people. And never would she forget the time he left school and got himself a job in the local Ironmongers and without prompting handed over a good portion of his small wage to her for his keep.

She was not too happy when he wrote to say he was training to be an air gunner. He wrote again when he joined a squadron as a tail gunner on a Halifax bomber. Strangely enough she didn't worry so much about the dangers of his work. She was more concerned about him making a fool of himself with the shortcomings in his education. Her information, gleaned from the newspapers and recruiting posters, gave the impression that aircrew were highly educated because of the dangerous and intelligent work they had to do.

And here was her son rubbing shoulders with his captain who had a double-barrelled name, which suggested he came from one of those high-fallutin families who lived in a big house, owned lots of land, and had an army of servants at their beck and call. Maurice had told her that it was this very officer who had got him his promotion to sergeant. Their navigator was also an officer and a gentleman, so Maurice claimed. He never pulled rank and always spoke to you, and not down as some snobby officers did. Then there was dear old Bosey, the daddy in the crew because he was the oldest. He had done much in the early days to help Maurice when he was raw and inexperienced. And, what was more, it was Bosey who had pulled them out of some very narrow scrapes. She mustn't worry, Maurice told her. He was in with the best and safest of the crews.

She was thinking how relieved she was to know Maurice was among a dependable, decent lot in the air force when Tom told Billy and Bella they could leave the table. She was in the throes of washing the dishes when the doorknocker sounded at the front of the house. "All right! I'll answer it." Tom called.

She worked on at the sink planning her evening. She would wash and salt the meat and prepare the vegetables for tomorrow's Sunday roast. She would make a jelly and custard and bake a few scones. Following that she would take to her easy chair by the hearth, with her knitting and listen to, 'At the Luscombes' on the radio, a family drama that she followed avidly. Later she would listen to, 'In Town Tonight' in which the rich and the famous notably of the theatre and cinema were interviewed. Her imagination showed the celebrities to be dressed in smart dinner suits and the ladies in white ermine coats, sparkling, dangling ear rings, beautifully styled hair, and they stood with wide, bright smiles in the glare of the studio lights and the flash bulbs of visiting photographers. She escaped for a few precious moments and shared the glamour and prestige of the stars, remote from her house and family. She fantasised for perhaps only about five minutes. But it was enough. Enough to spur her on and give her bit of a boost to face up to the forthcoming week and her duties as a wife and mother.

It suddenly occurred to her that Tom was spending a long time at the front door. She handed a tea towel to Bella, told her to finish drying, told Billy to refill the coal scuttle, and moved through the small sitting room into the tiny hall to find Tom sitting on the bottom step of the stairs, head hung low, holding a yellow piece of paper. He looked slowly up at her, pale-faced, shocked. He hauled himself up unsteadily using the stair bannister. "I think we ought to go upstairs, my dear."

She followed his slow, heavy tread up the stairs around the landing at the top into their bedroom. He closed the door behind them and for the first time in years he held both her hands. He said gravely, "You'd better brace yourself, Milly. I've got some bad news."

Milly was not one to show a lot of emotion herself. She could fly off the handle if unfairly provoked. But in the main she kept her more personal and sensitive feelings deep-rooted and out of sight.

"It's our Maurice, isn't it?" she said.

"Yes, I'm afraid it is, my dear." He coaxed her to sit on the bedside and placed an arm around her. She was glad about that; her legs had turned to jelly and her heart was beating more loudly than normal. She fought hard to find something to say to Tom to comfort him. His solemn expression and quivering lips told her that he was taking the news badly. She relieved him of the telegram and read:

WE REGRET YOUR SON SERGEANT MAURICE CLARKE IS MISSING ON OPERATIONS AND IS PRESUMED DEAD.

A part of her refused to believe it. His letters were always of a happy note and if he had told her once, he had told her at least twenty times, that he was flying with the best and safest crew in the squadron. And this had been supported by the fact they had gone out night after night and always came back.

Tom said: "Like to stay here whilst I get you a strong cup of tea?"

She nodded and held his hand, "Thank you, Tom. That would be nice. And a cigarette, please." She wasn't a great smoker. But there were occasions when it warranted its use. A cigarette and a cup of strong, sweet tea were the sure remedies, in her opinion, for coping with the emotional storms that life had occasion to inflict on an individual or a family.

When he had gone she allowed herself the privilege of shedding a few tears in private. And dried her eyes on the turned-down top sheet of her bed.

"Something's happened to our Maurice, hasn't it dad." Bella said as Tom walked into the kitchen.

"I'll tell you, later. For the time being make your mother a strong of tea. And I'll take it up to her."

Billy sat at the cleared kitchen table, working on a model aeroplane, made a similar enquiry. Tom ignored him and made an excuse to visit the outside lavatory. Where he remained until he thought the tea was ready.

When he returned upstairs his wife said: "Have you told Bella and Billy yet?"

"No, my dear." He looked perplexed. "I thought you'd do it better than me."

Poor, old Tom, Milly thought, grateful, to some extent, for his inadequacies. It diverted her thoughts from her own anxiety and made her take the part of the hen who would rally her brood when one of their number had been taken by a fox.

She took her time sipping at the tea and enjoying a cigarette. She found her thoughts drifting back to her childhood when her pet dog Sammy had been run over and killed by a car. She remembered her father taking her onto his lap, cuddling her and trying to comfort her. He tried to explain that sometimes these tragedies in our youth often came about for a reason. He didn't know why but very often that it was preparing us for something in the years ahead, he said.

Milly had never really understood what he meant. But now some thirty-five years later, and confronted by the loss of her son, she felt and knew exactly what the death and loss of her dog had prepared her for.

Samuel Herby sat in his office looking thoughtfully at a particular wall that was hidden behind a mass of photographs and paintings. In the centre hung a large oil painting of him standing by the kite that he had built and flown from Hadley in the old country all those years ago. He'd brought it to Canada when he first arrived with Rebecca and Timothy. Claire Hadley had painted it, as had she painted a studio portrait of Timothy in the uniform of a captain in the Royal Flying Corps. Another canvas portrayed their daughter, Samantha, dressed in white overalls, clutching her helmet and goggles, standing before a Moth biplane.

Beneath it was a framed photograph of his grandson, Paul, in his helmet and bulky Mae West smiling out from the cockpit of a Spitfire. Twelve swastikas were painted on the fuselage just aft of the engine bulkhead.

On each side of Paul in separate shots was Peter and Jaque dressed in flying togs. He had yet to meet them but already they were very special to him. He was certain they had a lot of Herby blood and, what was more, they had flying in their veins. Helen, his granddaughter, in a nearby picture, posed in a smart white, winged hat and the dark blue cloak of a nurse. He thought Rebecca would enjoy meeting her, although there wasn't much chance of that with the War on.

Surrounding the family pictures was a mass of smaller prints showing the flying students who had passed through his hands over the years. Most of them were now in Britain serving in the various commands of the Royal Air Force. A number had been decorated for their bravery and flying skills in fighters, bombers and aircraft of Coastal Command. A lot of them had perished like Samantha and Paul. He sighed heavily; it seemed such a waste of young potential.

He noticed Phoebe go past a nearby window and head for the main entrance doors to the building. She wore a woollen dress to her ankles under which she hid suede muclots and over which she exhibited a fur lined and fur trimmed Parka. She didn't walk; she glided along, back straight, head held high and the reddish brown countenance of her face, from her mixed origins, beaming out from the hood of her coat. Presently he heard her in the office next door and he visualised her removing her coat and changing her boots for moccasins. Next she moved back out and went down the corridor to the small kitchen to make coffee. After which she would bring the coffee, and the mail, to his office and they'd sit together and sort the letters. He was filling in for Bill Cornell who had taken a spot of leave.

There were envelopes containing Bills. There were letters to the students from their folk back home. There were letters to the chief engineer of the workshops. There were letters to instructors from their charges who had moved on to Advanced Flying Training or had graduated and reached operational squadrons in Britain and were now in the thick of the air war. Bill Cornell had three letters marked 'Private and Confidential'. Phoebe had a letter from her mother in Quebec and from her brother in Toronto. Samuel picked up a letter with a British postmark and whose hand writing on the envelope he recognised as that of his son, Timothy. He hoped the letter enclosed more snaps of the grandchildren. He slid a paper knife beneath the lapel to open it and withdrew a single sheet of military notepaper.

As he read the letter Phoebe noticed his face turn pale, the corners of his mouth and his moustache began to twitch and he clenched his right fist, which clearly showed his knuckles.

At the end of the letter his head drooped and he passed it to her, to read.

Epilogue

In November 1945 Brigadier Towers was among a great number of officers and men to be repatriated from Japanese prisoner-of-war camps. But such was his emaciated condition he spent nigh on six months in a military hospital receiving treatment to his many ailments, and being fattened up before the Army risked sending him home.

He arrived at his home in March 1946 still looking frightfully pale and frail and only half the man Majorie once knew. She opened the door to him and stood to attention and saluted him in greeting, smiling. Then she embraced his tall, gaunt form, "Welcome home, Gerald." She kissed him lightly on the face. He leaned heavily against her, proving how weak he was. She steadied him, took his bag and topcoat, and led him to an easy chair before a roaring, crackling hearth fire. That's when he broke down and wept.

Majorie sat on the arm of the chair and put a consoling arm around him.

"Please forgive me, my dear," he croaked. "For being absent all these years. I'm truly sorry."

She increased the grip of her arm around him. "You mustn't reproach yourself, Gerald. It was the war. And, now, it's all over, and we are back together again," She squeezed him again with her arm and added, "How would you like a whisky and soda to celebrate your return?"

He blinked at her through red-rimmed moist eyes and nodded. "May I have a double?"

"Certainly not!" she smiled. " Your rank entitles you to a treble."

Whilst she mixed the drinks he got up and removed his military tunic, loosened his tie and wiped his eyes and blew his nose. "My God!" he declared "It's so good to be home." He turned to find his wife holding a full glass.

"Here's to the future. OUR future!" Majorie nudged her glass against his.

"Our future!" he declared. And they drank to it.

At that moment a girl of about three years with red hair, twinkling brown eyes and a bright smile toddled into the room. The Brigadier looked bewildered almost alarmed.

Majorie said, "Come Willemena. Come and meet your foster father, Brigadier Towers."

The girl came and stood respectfully before him and put out a small hand in greeting. It did a little to placate his tumbling thoughts, his measure of unease. He took the hand and held it.

Majorie said, "Her father got killed on bombing operations. He was flying from Beeston, up the road. And her mother abandoned her. So I offered to take her in. I must confess she has been good company in your absence."

"Thank goodness for that." he sighed heavily. "I thought you were going to say," He paused. "No I mustn't say it."

"Say what, Gerald?"

"Well, you see my dear, it was revealed to us in hospital that many wives of the prisoners got so lonely in the prolonged absences of their husbands that they fell into the arms of other men. And many were made pregnant." He looked her steadily in the eye. "Do you remember Bunny Watson's wife – what was her name?"

"Oh, you mean Daphne."

"That's it. And you've not heard?"

"Heard what, Gerald?"

"She has had two children in his absence; each one by a different father. The poor man is devastated. On the verge of suicide they say."

Majorie avoided the delicate subject and said, "What about some food! Anything special you fancy?"

"Do I have a choice? He said. " I thought you were on rations."

"We are." She smiled. " But I've built up a little stock of most things."

He said, "Make a suggestion."

"Well, if I remember rightly you were rather partial to my Cottage Pies, Bangers and Mash, and Macaroni Cheese."

"And," he licked his lips. " Your dashing steak and kidney pies."

"So, what's it to be?"

"May I have macaroni cheese today. And the pie tomorrow."

She left him talking with Willamena and busied herself in the kitchen. It gave her some breathing space. Her daughter was a constant reminder of Teddy. She had his colour hair and eyes. And like him, and her, she had a lively intellect. Majorie adored her. She never regretted for a moment her indiscretion with Teddy. It had given her an opportunity to prove herself as a woman and produce an offspring.

Willamena toddled into the kitchen and said, "Daddy Brigadier would like another whisky, please Mumsy."

Majorie was in the middle of making the cheese sauce. "Tell Daddy Brigadier to help himself, my darling. I might burn the cooking."

On the approach to Christmas that year Jaque Bosanquet arrived in the West Country. He parked his car in a country lane alongside a stone wall that belonged to the front yard of a rather charming, elegant farmhouse. There was something warm and welcoming about the place with its stone clad walls, latticework windows, red tiled roof and smoke curling up from its chimney pots. He'd been on the road for four hours, travelling from Kent, except for a twenty-minute stop mid point of the journey to buy petrol and take refreshment. He got out of the car, lit a cigarette and stood taking in the view of the surrounding countryside. Fields and dividing hedgerows sloped away to a small hamlet in one direction. A majestic church spire probed the skyline beyond a gathering of trees. A train of hilly contours posed as another view. Whilst to the west the land ran flat for several miles before rising again.

He opened the five-barred gate and was greeted by a couple of playful black and white Collies. He stroked and patted them for a spell to calm them. And they followed him to the front porch.

The door opened to an elderly lady wearing a floral printed pinafore and who had a duster bulging from a pocket.

"I'm visiting Mrs Hadley-Chase and her family," Bosey said.

"I'm afraid she and her husband are away for a few days, sir. I'll get her daughter-in-law."

Jenny came to the door and on seeing him threw her arms around him, "Jaque!" she cried. "How lovely to see you. Come in! Come in!" Contrary to everyone else she always called him by his Christian name and she pronounced it with French accent. He had returned her, pregnant with the twins, back to the farm and her in laws shortly after Peter lost his life. And they'd kept in touch by letter ever since.

Over a period of time his letters had helped her to come to terms with her grief and gradually her thoughts and feelings began to focus on Jaque. Although it had to be said that throughout his letter writing he had never intimated that their relationship was anything more than platonic.

As they embraced each other she couldn't avoid pressing against him and feeling his face against hers. She enjoyed the warmth and security in the fold of his arms. "It's so good to see you, Jaque," she whispered and kissed him fully on the lips.

By the same token it was a long time since the pilot had held a woman in his arms. He savoured her closeness and the pulse of life that passed between them as they held each other. He found the attraction both strong and natural.

Presently Jenny invited him in, took his hat and coat, and led him through to the sitting room where two children amused each other in a playpen. "Samuel and Polly," she announced. "The boy named after his great grandfather, and the girl after my mother."

Whilst she fed and bathed the children he drove the cleaning lady to her home near the railway station for Jenny. When he got back Jenny was talking to the farm manager who reported each day to the family: the milk yield, what staff were listed in the milk parlour for the following day and other bits of information concerning the sheep, and the cream and cheese production.

Later he and Jenny played with the children in their bedroom for a time and Bosey delighted them all, including Jenny, by reading a couple of bedtime stories. Within minutes two rosy faces with closed eyes and tousled hair rested snugly on their pillows, breathing evenly in sleep.

Whilst Jenny heated lamb stew and dumplings for supper he fetched a bag from his car had a shave and changed into cords and a casual shirt. They ate in the kitchen and Jenny broached a bottle of homemade Elderberry wine and treated him to a lemon meringue for a dessert.

They washed and dried the dishes and cutlery together. Then moved to the sitting room where a log fire burned cheerily in a large hearth. Jenny switched off the main ceiling light and the room bathed in the soft yellow glow of two table lamps. She drew up beside him on the settee before the hearth and said: "So what have you been doing since you left the air force, Jaque?"

He said, "I've been visiting the relatives and friends of Peter's crew who, as you may recall, flew with me for half the tour of operations. I felt I had a duty to check up on the girls they left behind to see how they were faring."

She turned to him, smiling, "That was most thoughtful of you, Jaque. How were they all?" She remembered them from the times she and Peter held parties at the cottage at Beeston and they all came along, Peter's crew and the ground crew and their lady friends. They played Charades and Sardines and generally made merry. They danced to music from a gramophone. Sometimes they danced in the garden under the stars. Regularly they performed a conga, which invariably involved climbing up and over the roof of the cottage and, on several occasions, snaking up into the branches of the apple tree that stood in the middle of the garden. "Six months of sheer, unstoppable fun." Jenny said wistfully. " I doubt if I'll see anything like it again."

Bosey said, "Do you remember Wilf Walters in the crew? He was the bombaimer."

"Oh, yes. The Welshman with that beautiful, rich baritone voice."

"And do you remember, Majorie, his lady friend?"

"Yes. She was a bit older than he was, if I remember rightly. She adored him, didn't she?"

Bosey turned to look at her. "Did you know she was married to an army Brigadier who ended up as a Japanese POW?"

"Really!"

"And she also had a baby by Wilf."

"No! I never heard anything about that. Goodness, gracious, Jaque, you must tell me about it."

He said, " From what I was told, Majorie was a teacher by profession. And Wilf came from a family of schoolteachers. That's why, I presume, they hit it off. Wilf came into her life when she was approaching an age where she was having grave doubts about ever producing a family, particularly as her husband was out of reach for an indefinite period in the POW camp. She took to Wilf's young, strong and intelligent pedigree, and decided he'd make an ideal candidate for fatherhood."

" And he obviously fulfilled that role?"

"Oh, yes. He gave her a daughter, a charming and lively girl who has his red hair, twinkling brown eyes and impish smile. Majorie adores her."

"What happened to her husband? Did he survive the war? And, if so, how did Majorie explain her situation when he came home."

Bosey said: "She's a remarkable woman. I visited her three weeks ago. And there she was, calm and in total control. A proud mother and a great nurse to her husband who is slowly regaining his physical strength and mental alacrity under her dedicated care. During my visit she found an excuse for him to play with the daughter in the garden. And that's when she told me, in his absence, that he had come to accept the mantle of foster father thinking, as Majorie had told him, her father was an airman from Beeston who lost his life on active service and the mother was a local woman who abandoned her.

Majorie is quite convinced that it was her destiny to conceive her daughter as she did. She wrote to Wilf's parents to let them know of their granddaughter, having got their address from the last letter he left on his bedside locker, prior to setting out on the last operation, marked 'To be opened in the event of my death'. He left two letters in fact. One to his parents and one to Majorie."

"How did Majorie's husband take to that? Surely he must have suspected something fishy was going on."

"Majorie told him they were the parents of Willamena's father who had been killed on operations from Beeston. Which was quite true. Then when the Brigadier inquired about the existence of the grandparents on the mother's side of the family, Majorie reminded him of the mother's abandonment of Willlamena and the fact she had disappeared without trace."

"Goodness gracious, Jaque! This is getting intriguing. How did Wilf's parents receive the news of their granddaughter?"

Bosanquet said, "Evidently Wilf's father, a staunch Chapel man, was not too pleased about the adultery aspect of the relationship. He also felt their sins would visit the head of their offspring. But Wilf's mother and brothers accepted the news with delight. When I was there last, Majorie was planning a visit to Wales with Willamena."

Jenny frowned. "How did Majorie register the birth? That must have given her a few scruples."

"No, I don't think so. She was quite honest about it all. She named Wilf as the father and used her maiden name as the mother: a suggestion put to her by her midwife."

Jenny moved and threw three more logs on the fire. After a short period of hissing and crackling from the expanding, splitting wood the reflection of the flames danced on the surrounding walls. She poured two glasses of sherry and took them to the settee. And Bosey lit two cigarettes and handed her one. They sat for a short while in silence. She drew closer to him and tried not to make it look too obvious.

Bosey said, "Do you remember Maurice Clarke in the crew?" He was the mid upper gunner. Then later flew as the radio operator when the turret was removed from the Halifax."

"Oh yes, Maurice. Such a smart and polite boy, I remember. Peter said he was the youngest in the crew and yet he was the tallest."

"He was."

Jenny said, "His girlfriend, I recall, was rather reticent and shy at times. But always beautifully dressed. Was she a local girl? I never did find out. Gloria wasn't it?"

Bosey said cautiously "Yes, that's right. There was something of a tragedy about her. But only a very few people knew about it."

Jenny stirred and looked around into his face. " Tragedy! What tragedy, Jaque?"

"Gloria was what you might say, a freak of nature."

Jenny frowned heavily, "I didn't notice that she had a disability or an impediment in her speech. Or anything like. If anything I thought her quite bright."

"She was. Her affliction, if you could call it that, was more biological."

Jenny's feminine curiosity got the better of her, "Come now!" She urged him. "What are you trying to tell me?"

"Well, you said earlier that you'd been unable to find out if she was a local girl."

"That's right."

Bosey looked at her sympathetically, "Gloria was, in fact Sergeant Clarence Stanton, a male nurse at Beeston."

"But that's preposterous, Jaque. Gloria was an out and out woman. Her hair, her breasts and her shapely legs – how I envied those legs. I even caught Maurice kissing her in the garden during one of our riotous parties and she yielded in his arms like any young woman." She paused and turned to him, a frown masking her face "If what you say is true then Maurice must have been either very naïve or peculiar to have been in love with her."

Bosey said, "You can't really accuse him of that, Jenny. After all said and done you wouldn't have known had I not told you. And not once during all those parties at the cottage, did I notice anyone suspect that she was anything rather than a very attractive woman."

Jenny, somewhat agitated, went and refilled their glasses with Sherry.

She sat down beside him and said, "It's all rather grotesque when you think about it. That person, a guest at all of our private parties, duping us into thinking she was a woman. Do you know I took her into my confidence on a number of occasions and we spoke about womanly things. And, now, I feel such a fool at thinking that all the time I was disclosing my private matters to her, when she was, in fact, a man."

Bosey said, " She was born as female gender so the story goes. But shortly into her life she tragically developed a male organ."

"But that's absolutely cruel, Jaque. How did you find out about this?"

"He came to my quarters on the night Peter and his crew went down. He'd found out from Operations that D-Dog had failed to return and he wanted to know if I knew anything. Of course his main concern was Maurice Clark.

I took him inside my room and told him what I knew. He grew very distraught and wept for a good ten minutes. So I made him a strong mug of tea and gave him a cigarette. And that's when he confessed to being Gloria at your parties, and Maurice's partner. Then he told me about his dual gender and his freak anatomy."

Jenny said, "What happened to him after that?"

" I never saw him again because, if you remember from my letters, I was posted away from Beeston to that Heavy Conversion Unit as an instructor. However, in my recent travels I visited Maurice's parents in Doncaster. And what do I find? A framed photograph of Gloria next to Maurice proudly displayed on a sideboard. She looked resplendent in a lilac coloured costume of skirt and jacket, white lace gloves and a white wide-brimmed hat. Maurice's parents regarded her as a very pretty girl and had convinced themselves that she came from a good family. They were very proud, particularly his mother, when Maurice wrote home to say they had become engaged and he would be bringing Gloria home to meet them on his next leave."

Jenny said urgently, enthusiastically, "Did she ever meet the Clarke family?"

"No. Maurice was killed before he got the chance to take her home. She wrote regularly to Mrs Clarke, even after the war ended. But she was so tied up running a hospice for the terminally ill she claimed she couldn't find the time to visit them.

Then quite out of the blue, a couple of weeks before my last visit, they received a letter from her in which she said the hospice had closed down due to a lack of funds. She had recently undergone some rather delicate surgery and was about to embark upon a new life in Africa with a Mr Martin Chopper, an eminent surgeon, who was pioneering unusual surgical techniques. She said that she was likely to be kept very busy in her new environment and therefore her letters might become few and far between: a hint that the correspondence would eventually fizzle out."

Jenny's feminine curiosity seized on the drama and said, " What d'you think her surgery was for?"

Bosey said, "I could be totally wrong. But I can't help thinking that Mr Chopper removed her male organ, dabbling as he does in that type of surgery, and converted her back to the full status of a woman. But one thing I did find odd and that was after receiving all this news about the surgery and Gloria's new life with the surgeon the Clarke's did not remove her photograph from the sideboard.

.Jenny shrugged, "They probably had their reasons." Then she said, "Talking about the other girlfriends of the crew, what happened to the girl who David Croker brought along to the parties? She struck me as a smart, ambitious girl. Fiona, wasn't it?"

"Yes. She got her commission in the end you know, at the fifth time of applying. I was at Beeston a few weeks back and she told me that the ending of the war was likely to stifle any further promotion prospects for her. So she was seriously thinking of leaving the air force and looking for a job."

Jenny said, " I think she'd go far in civilian life" She is so determined. And without appearing snobbish I thought she had more up top than the rear gunner."

Bosey said, "She had more initiative that's for sure. But Davey Croker had a big chip on his shoulder. That was his problem. Fiona came along and got rid of that and a lot of his rough edges and succeeded in making something of him. In fact, from what I could make out, she got him interested in going to church with her and taking Holy Communion."

"My goodness! Did she?"

"Yes. And they intended to get married at the end of his tour."

Jenny said sadly. "What actually was his background? Where did he come from?"

"Liverpool from what I know. He only ever mentioned a mother, never a father, to Fiona. He said she was a street woman and for years she dumped him on a lot of families. He was eventually taken in by the church welfare who got him a job, after he left school, working with an Undertakers. Fiona told me she has tried to contact the mother through all the Churches in Liverpool. But without success."

Jenny said, "All this gossip has made me a bit peckish, Jaque. How about a round of ham sandwiches and a mug of Ovaltine?"

" Are you sure I'm not boring you?"

"Not at all. It's all very intriguing." She went off to the kitchen.

When she returned they sat in silence for a time enjoying the food and drink in the flickering light of the hearth and feeling the heat reaching their legs and faces.

"Did you ever meet Harvey Fenton's people?" she said

"Yes. As a matter of fact I did. I was at his parent's home, in Surrey, only last week. I don't think either of them will ever recover from the loss of Harvey."

"I can quite understand it." Jenny said. "Harvey was every parent's ideal of a son. Handsome, modest, intelligent and a good ambassador for the family. I thought him a rather lonely person in that he didn't seem very interested in the ladies. Or was he just shy?"

Bosey grinned and said, "Harvey liked the ladies all right; preferably of the very young variety. Her name was Kate. Harvey was five years her senior. They lived in neighbouring houses and grew up together. He taught her to ride a bicycle and she got her first swimming lesson from him. During school holidays they went off on cycling expeditions to the lake at Frizling where they had picnics and swam among the dinghies of the sailing club.

He also helped her prepare for her entrance exams to a private school. And further assisted her with her homework when she gained a place at the school.

She was one of those girls who developed early, physically and mentally, and she was only eleven years of age when she reached puberty. She found herself suddenly and physically drawn to Harvey. There were times, now, in each month of her life when the yearning became a craving, an urgent, feverish demand for him to mate with her and rid her of the final barrier that separated the woman from the girl. It irked her that her parents continued to treat her as a girl when, in her mind, all her emotions were those of a young woman. She had a great urge to break free and be independent. She wanted to get rid of her school uniform and those awful white ankle-socks and wear a stylish dress and stockings. She had arguments with her parents about it and her rebellious streak met with a lot of opposition both at home and school. At one stage she got very close to being expelled from school around her twelfth birthday.

She had Harvey to thank, for coming to rescue her from a very fraught and volatile time in her young life. He took her for a long walk of an evening and he came up with a great idea as a compromise. He would buy her a dress, stockings and the black, patent, high heel shoes, and adult lingerie she desperately wanted, and he would take her dancing at the Cressida in Kingston. But if he were to get her parents permission to take her dancing she would have to agree to the school regulations and the other wishes of her parents.

Harvey took her home and negotiated the deal and healed the rift by getting them all to shake hands and promise a fresh start.

From hereon when not attending school she dressed as she wished. She and Harvey took dancing lessons and they did indeed make it to the Cressida when she was under age. But by now her breasts were large and firm, there was hair upon her body and her legs were shapely. Her lips were full, red and eager to be kissed. And like the rose in full bloom she desired to be plucked.

She gave Harvey the honour of removing her virginity and they became regular lovers. They made love in her bedroom when her parents were next doors playing cards with Harvey's parents. They made love in the summerhouse at the bottom of her garden where they rendezvoused after dark and their parents had retired for the night. They also crept out in the night and Harvey rode her on the crossbar of his bike to the lake at Frizling. Where they swam in the nude, made love on the grassy banks, drank wine and generally enjoyed that intoxication of passion and romance that only comes with the vigour and novelty of youth."

"How old was she?" Jenny broke in the conversation.

"From what she told me, she was about twelve or thirteen at the time. And Harvey was between seventeen, eighteen."

"That's very young for a girl. Didn't she ever worry about falling for a child?"

"By all accounts Harvey took precautions. That was – up to the last time he went on leave. Then they got married by special license."

"What age was she then?"

"Sixteen. And she claimed that she conceived at Harvey's first unprotected shoot."

Jenny said, " That's very young. What is she doing these days?"

"She still lives with her parents. She visits her in-laws every day and her son is named after Harvey. Her mother insists she had grown up too fast and missed a lot of her childhood. But Kate says that's nonsense. She said it was, of course, very sad to lose Harvey but that she would have had a lot more regrets had she and Harvey not indulged in the manner that they had. She also maintained that it was the intimate nature of the relationship with Harvey that made her more mature, and made her take her school studies more seriously. She eventually graduated from her private school with no less than seven certificates." Bosey paused and looked at Jenny. "She has plans to train as a teacher. And she asked for your address because she knew Harvey and Peter were very close. She has a very good photograph of them standing together before a Halifax, dressed for an operation. I'd not seen it before."

Jenny stifled a yawn with a hand and as she made to check the time by her wristwatch the grandfather clock in the hall struck ten times.

"Bedtime?" he said

"Not quite. Just one more before we retire, please Jaque. Sergeant Edwards! He looked after the engines, I remember Peter telling me."

"That's right. I visited his parents in Kent. They were very philosophical about their son's death. They said it was the way he would have wanted to go. All they wanted to know, was it quick. And I told them it was quick as a flash, which it was.

The odd thing that did intrigue them was Joyce, Eddy's girlfriend. Do you remember her from the parties?"

"Yes, I do. A dark hair, vivacious woman."

Bosey said: "She wrote to Eddy's people just the once, after he was killed, and explained that she felt very guilty and something of a jinx. She'd had a relationship with three flight engineers, at different times; having been married to the second one, Eddy's best friend, and all three had lost their lives. She did actually put in a surprise visit to the Edwards just after the war ended in Europe. She was married to a Church of England vicar by that time and they had a son, Kenneth, named after the Edwards son. They weren't that impressed. They'd always wanted their son to marry Kay, a Kent girl, and a friend of the family. But, of course, he never did." Bosey stood and took her hands and pulled her up. "Come now. Your bed awaits you." He led her across the room and put her in front and followed her up the stairs.

The sky had lost its azure tint of summer and its tempered blue of autumn. It portrayed the icy blue of the deepening winter. Clouds came in a flurry and passed overhead in a hurry driven by a biting, chilling northeasterly wind. Bosey wore his old fleece-lined Irvin flying jacket with his old woolen school scarf wound double around his neck, air force blue trousers and a pair of suede brogues. The only civilian clothes he owned were the ones the air force gave him when he was demobbed. Jenny walked in step, an arm interlocked with his. She wore a woolen scarf over her head and had an end wrapped around her face and draped over her shoulder Her coat was three quarter length, part of her Land Army uniform. Mittens warmed her hands and long subtle leather riding boots heated her legs and feet. They were running the dogs whilst the daily help cared for the children.

They moved out of the wind and walked in the lee of a line of tall Hawthorn and felt a little heat from the sun. They slowed their pace and Jenny said, "What do you intend to do now that you're out of the air force, Jaque?" She was curious to know if she featured in any of his plans.

"I'm off to Canada in January."

"Canada!" She succeeded in not screaming the word and made every effort to make it sound casual and just a little surprised. Canada was a long way away and it looked as if he was going out of her life when he had only been back in it for a day.

"My father, and Peter's, the wing commander you met at Beeston, has booked a passage for me to return with him and his wife to Canada to meet my grandfather who is eager to meet me. He's not in very good health and, from what I gather, he wants to discuss something very urgently."

"How long will you stay in Canada?" She posed the question, hoping desperately that he was not going to say he was staying indefinitely.

"Nobody has really said. A month at least, I would have thought. It's quite a distance to go and stay for only a few days."

"And what then, Jaque? After you come back from Canada?" She fought down the desperation that was creeping into her voice. The loneliness and the deprivation that had accompanied her since Peter's death and which had been kept at bay to some extent by letters from Jaque, and then almost abrogated by his present visit, seemed suddenly to rear its unfriendly face.

He paused to light two cigarettes and gave her one. "I plan to go back to Croydon and restart my garage business that was bombed out during the war."

"You had your own business?"

He nodded. "And a house. And a family."

Jenny recoiled and drew a deep breath from the shock of his revelation and tears misted her eyes. She tried to comprehend what he meant by a house and a family. In all the time she had known him and exchanged correspondence, not once had it been mentioned She stopped walking, withdrew her arm from his and took a hankie from a pocket and wiped her eyes and runny nose. She looked at him, trembling. "Are you telling me, after all the time we have known one another, and the letters we have sent to each other, that you are married?"

He said, "I WAS married and had two daughters. They all died along with my mother during the early blitz on London. The house and my garage next door got a direct hit. I was on my first tour of operations at the time"

Jenny's collapsed against him with relief and wrapped her arms around him, "Oh my God, Jaque! Why didn't you ever tell me?"

He said, "I've never told anybody about it, except to report it to the Air Force records department."

"You mean you've carried the burden of this tragedy with you throughout the war? The strain must have been enormous."

He said reflectively, " It would have been nothing short of hypocrisy to take my tale of woe to anyone, including you, and condemn the Germans for killing my mother, wife and children. When, in fact, I was doing exactly the same thing, killing women and children, during the nightly raids on German towns and cities."

Jenny made to contest it by saying the Germans had started the war and that he had every right to retaliate.

He said: "Don't let's get involved in the politics of war. I'm not a politician and I never want to be. My father told me that the Herby family, from which I'm descended, is by inclination pioneers, not warriors. They are also patriotic and that is why they are drawn to offer their services when their mother country is ever threatened. I suppose I've got a bit of it in the genes but also a dash of French blood. I don't recall going to war to fight for my country. I went to war because I could fly. And that's all I wanted to do, as did previous Herby generations."

Jenny said, " Peter was uneasy about the war. He never liked to talk about it in depth. He preferred to talk about the characters in his crew. And, of course, like you and the Herby family he enjoyed describing the spectacular moments in the flying itself. The clear sunlit sky, the armies of cloud, the counterpanes of cloud, stormy, turbulent air that pounced unseen on a machine. And those dim, starry, tranquil skies at night. He spoke about the type of journeys they made to, and back home, from a target. But he never mentioned the dropping of the bombs."

Bosey did not comment; he eased her to one side, put her arm through his and carried on walking. They came to a stile leading to a bridal path. In one flowing movement he lifted her bodily and placed her over the stile. She derived a good deal of pleasure from the strength of his hold and his touch. They broke out of the lee of the tall Hawthorn bushes and immediately the cold north wind made her eyes water. She wiped them with the back of a mitten and said, "Will you rebuild the garage and the house?"

"I'll need to go to the Council or Corporation first to talk about the plans and ask if they'll finance the rebuild. Then I need to find a Bank to borrow some money to get some working capital. I'd like to have some petrol pumps as part of the business this time. I don't intend to rebuild the house. I think a flat built above the garage would be more economical."

"Will you run it on your own?"

"It depends. I had a retired Brooklands mechanic working for me before the war and up to the time it was bombed. I'd like to get him back if he's still around. And I also had a lad, Chirpy Warbler we called him. He got called up when war broke out. I wouldn't mind having him back here when he comes out of the army, if he should still be alive."

Jenny stopped him walking and held his hands, "You don't have to tell me if you'd rather not, or, if it's too painful. But tell me about your wife and children."

There's not much to tell really. There was Monique, my French wife, and our two daughters Rosana and Fleur. That's about it."

"Are you French?"

"Half and half. English father, French mother

"Everyone called you Bosey at Beeston. I always thought that was a nickname."

"Bosey was short for Bosanquet. My mother's maiden name."

"Was she pretty?"

"As a flower. Petite also. But volatile as a bee."

Jenny smiled, " Did she have a sting?"

"Only if you mentioned my father. Then she'd sting you hard with her tongue. All because he wouldn't marry her when she fell pregnant with me. It turns out his squadron -this happened in the First World War mind you – got orders to move at short notice. He crept out of his camp, without permission, to let her know. She tells him she is pregnant and expects the war to stop for them to marry, which of course it can't. From what she told me there was a big scene and she asked him to leave and get out of her life. He tried to make amends again at the end of the war by visiting her home in France. But she had moved to England with me by this time and is living with a disabled British Army officer. My father again tried to help her. But she refused to let him cross the threshold of her door and sent him away with another flea in his ear. He never tried again."

"So you grew up in England?"

"Yes. Mother never married the army officer. He died quite early after the end of the war from mustard gas poisoning. I can still remember him coughing almost non-stop up to the time of his death, poor fellow. He left my mother the cottage and a small amount of money in his will. We moved to Croydon, after she sold the cottage, and lived in a small French quarter that had sprung up there."

"How did she cope, bringing you up single-handed?"

"She took in laundry and ironing and also gave private piano lessons. She was never short of customers. I remember so clearly people coming and going with baskets and bundles. And on rainy days every room in our small house had line strung across it with clothes hung up to dry. It got a bit cramped and damp at times." He paused. "But otherwise we lived comfortably. Mother cared for me well and I went to a happy school.

When I left school I went to work as a trainee mechanic in a local garage and mother, in the main, was happy and content. Until the day I announced I wanted to learn to fly. I had been working in the garage for three years at that point. The war was only about three years away and the Royal Air Force were putting advertisements in the newspapers and on bill boards inviting men to join the Volunteer Reserve and train as pilots and observers."

Mother said adamantly, "Non, non, non, Jaque. It is not for you. Your father was an aviator and a disaster to us. Non, non, non, you be good boy and finish your training as a mechanic."

Jenny stopped him walking, smiling, her eyes still smarting from the icy wind. The sun had gone and the stars were out. "And did you?" she said.

"Yes. I carried on at the garage. But at weekends I attended the VR establishments when she thought I was visiting friends. I learnt to fly on Tiger Moths at White Waltham and travelled there by motor cycle. That went on for about a year. Then I got sent to a place called Watchfield to train on the Airspeed Oxford a twin-engine machine. When I was presented with my wings the war was about a year away. That year was busy for me. I started up my own garage and married Monique which was arranged by my mother as you can possibly imagine."

Jenny said, "Your mother had quite an influence on your life, didn't she?"

"She liked to think she had. And I made it look as if I was conforming to her wishes. But I normally got my own way because I was discreet. I never argued with her and never threw anything in her face. I just got on and did it. And the first time she knew anything about flying being a part of my life was when I dressed in full uniform and she spotted my winged brevet. I think I was attending a military parade that weekend. It brought tears to her eyes. She held my face in her hands kissed me on the brow and said, "Mon aviateur! Vous et tres admirable. Mais vous et plus moins votre le Pere."

"What did it mean?"

Bosey grinned, "She said: I was her admirable aviator. And that I was better looking than my father."

Jenny smiled, " How did you meet Monique?"

"She lived in the French quarter, a couple of streets from us. Mother met her through the Church and brought her home and introduced her to me. And one thing led to another. She was a good wife and mother but I regret I did neglect her. Not intentionally of course, but I was tied up a lot in the first place building up the garage business. And most weekends I was away training with the Volunteer Reserve. Then the War came and I was summoned to the regular air force."

"But you found time to conceive the children?" Jenny suggested with a smile.

"I had my mother constantly reminding me of my duties in that direction. And Monique, in typical French fashion, simply ushered me into the boudoir, lashed me to the bed ends and took her fill of me."

Jenny cocked an eyebrow in disbelief at the disclosure of his private life. Then, unable to contain herself and confronted by the cheeky expression on his face, she burst out laughing. "Was it really like that, Jaque?"

"I'll let you decide," he said. Then more seriously, "My mother was visiting Monique and the children on the night they were killed. From what the local air raid warden told me, she had got them all down into the air raid shelter in the garden. And that's what got a direct hit and the blast from, which blew the back of the house out. Another bomb scored a direct hit on the garage."

Jenny stopped him walking, held both his hands and faced him. "I'm truly sorry Jaque. I just don't know what else to say. I only wish you had told me all this before."

The quay at Southampton docks thronged with people who had come to see their relatives and friends off on the voyage. They huddled together and shuffled around to keep warm. Beneath their feet a layer of snow gradually turned to sludge persuaded, as it was, by the salty sea air. Just outside the docks in the Municipal parks the unaffected snow lay thick and permanent.

Jenny saw him come to the rail of the veranda on the third deck and wave down at her and Mollie and Horace. She waved energetically back up at him. He looked so different in mufti; she had only ever seen him in uniform previous to his recent arrival at the farm. He was dressed in a dark blue overcoat and black bowler hat and had a small white polka dot blue tie in the collar of his white shirt. They had rushed around in recent days to find a draper to get a dinner suit his size that his father had telephoned to say he would need for dining on board ship.

Jenny had done all his laundry and packed his small trunk in preparation for the voyage.

He had stayed at the farm for Christmas and New Year and they had had a glorious time in the company of Horace and Mollie and the children. They went to church on Christmas Eve' for midnight mass, just him and her, whilst Mollie and Horace cared for the children.

In the chilly darkness of the quay she bathed in a glow of happiness and contentment at recalling New Year's Eve' when Mollie and Horace hosted a dinner party at the farm and invited the farm hands and their spouses. A number of neighbours also came in the form of the local pastor and his wife: Harold Fowler, the local GP and his wife Miriam: a retired colonel who was a widower and a couple of unmarried sisters who ran the village grocery shop. The rest of the village celebrated en masse at the Cock and Arrow, the village inn.

Jenny was kept busy that day with the preparations. She and Jaque helped Mollie and Horace prepare the food and lay the large table in the hall during the afternoon. In the evening they waited on the table, insisting that Mollie and Horace dine with their guests.

In between the courses, in the privacy of the kitchen, they drank sherry and she grew a little merry. She stood on tip toe kissed him boldly and wished him Merry Christmas. She rather hoped he would respond and indicate in some way that he valued her presence in his life. But at that moment her mother-in-law interrupted to tell them they could serve the final course of biscuits and cheese.

The party grew more boisterous as the evening wore on. After dinner they pushed the chairs back in the sitting room and Horace plied a radiogram with records of music and song. They danced around the room without shoes.

At midnight they stopped to listen to the radio and linked arms and sang the traditional song to say farewell to the old year and welcome in the New. Then everybody was shaking hands, embracing, kissing and exchanging greetings of the New Year.

Horace always made a large pot of broth for the occasion and served it with crusty bread spread with a thick layer of butter. The guests took to a chair and Jenny and Bosey waited on them with the steaming bowls and the appetising smell of freshly baked bread.

About an hour after midnight the guests took their leave, adequately wined and dined and grateful to their hosts for their hospitality. Jenny sent Mollie and Horace on to bed and she and Jaque completed the washing and drying of the dishes and cutlery and tidied the sitting room where they opened the windows for a spell and emptied the ashtrays.

It was a little after two in the morning when Bosey surprised her by announcing he was taking a bit of fresh air before turning in.

"It's very late Jaque," she laughed and followed him into the hall where he trod into his suede flying boots and donned his leather sheepskin flying jacket and wound his old, woolen school scarf around his neck. He turned to her and surprised her even more when he said, "I'd like you to come with me."

"But it's very late. The farm breakfast is only three hours away."

He grinned at her, "We'll be back by then."

She donned a suede coat and a wooly hat, threw a scarf around her neck and trod into soft leather boots.

Out of doors the stars sparkled competitively and a full moon illuminated the snow-covered countryside with its eerie light. Jenny had not seen anything quite so beautiful. Everything was clean and pure in its presentation. And the silence! Nothing stirred except for the sound of their boots padding softly on the snow and they exhaled small clouds of condensation as they walked.

"How far are we going?" she said. She accidentally slipped and gripped his arm to recover. He steadied her and said, "Up to the crossroads. Then we'll head back."

When they reached the crossroad which, was on a little rise they could see in every direction. To the north the snow-covered hills looked like a gathering of heaped clouds resting on the horizon. To the west it was like a huge white eiderdown draped upon the earth with the hedgerow boundaries appearing as the black stitching that marked the seams of the panels. Southwards they could see the farmhouse, the moonlight glinting on the glass of the windows. It stood in visual repose, smoke rising vertically from the chimney pots, courtesy of the windless night. They turned and looked to the east where they could see the black needlepoint of the church spire dominating the skyline. He positioned himself behind her and put his arms around her waist. They came warm and comforting and secure and she was very aware of how much she wanted him to be part of her life. He held his face against her face. And when he spoke his words came to her, on the dark crystal of the night, like music to her ears and as balm to the fluttering uncertainty of her thoughts. He said gently, "I would like us to get married when I return from Canada, Jenny. If that's all right with you?"

On reflection of that moment Jenny wiped the tears of joy from her eyes and waved up to him again standing at the rail of the ship. And he waved back. He stood between his father and Marie who had been interviewed and filmed by Pathe News, a little earlier, along with a number of other celebrities before they went up the gangway to the ship.

As Marie Herby she had established herself as a concert pianist, after her son, Paul, was killed on flying operations. For the last year she had toured the bombed towns and cities in Britain giving her IN MEMORIAM concerts which she dedicated to all those mothers who had lost children in the war. She also featured on the light programme in concert with the BBC Symphony Orchestra.

The total experience gave her a new poise and confidence. And according to Horace it had helped her finally heal the rift that had existed for many years between her and Mollie, Peter's mother. Horace avoided going into detail regarding the reasons for the rift and merely said that the healing process started when Peter got killed. Having both lost a son to the war now gave them something in common and brought them closer together. Jenny had seen them earlier, embracing, smiling and shaking hands in farewell.

Three short blasts from the ship's siren interrupted her thoughts. The numerous portholes in the hull and the decks towering up before her began to slide forward and ease away from the quay. Suddenly a flurry of snowflakes enveloped the liner. It moved out of range of the quayside lighting and featured as a large tall phantom drifting eerily to the midstream of the channel, gradually disappearing from sight behind the curtain of falling snow. Overhead the cut diamonds of the stars came to view, sparkling on the unmolested blue velvet of the night sky.

For a long time the three of them stood in silence looking into the darkness. The quayside was almost deserted. The north wind came at them in small, icy gusts. Horace turned and led them from the quay and out of the docks. They turned up the High Street and headed for the Dolphin hotel where they were staying over night.

Across the Atlantic Ocean and several hundred miles further on across Canada to Calgary Samuel Herby rummaged about in the loft space of his home. The space covered the whole top of the house and as he moved about he could be heard in the rooms below. The wooden rafters creaked and groaned and occasionally disturbed the plaster ceiling on the other side and it fell on the bedroom furniture as a very fine powder. Rebecca was drawn from sleep by the noises, which were magnified by the deep silence of the night. She threw on a dressing gown and walked out of the bedroom and along the landing to the loft ladder, "What in Heaven's name are you doing up there, Samuel? Do you realise it's only three hours after midnight?"

His face appeared at the loft entrance, grinning, "I'm looking for the flags to hang out for the children to welcome them home."

" But they're not due for another ten days."

"Quite so my dear. But as you are often reminding me, don't leave for tomorrow what you can do today," he said and disappeared back inside the loft.

Rebecca turned away smiling. She had walked once again into her own trap and she only had herself to blame. But determined as ever to have the last word she said, "Don't forget you also have a duty to your wife, Samuel Herby. I'm waiting!" She hurried to the bedroom and was greeted by a cracking sound and a fall of plaster as a foot in a slipper and a leg in pajamas came crashing down through the ceiling.

IN MEMORIAM

'Their name liveth for evermore'
Hadley-Chase Flt. Lt. R.A.F. Remembering
with pride our son, Peter, and his
gallant crew killed on operations
29th Nov. 1943

Molly & Timothy

WINGS UPON THE NIGHT